# TOUGH

"Do – do you see—" jerked a trembling finger across the cafeteria at the back of Jordan's head, unable to control herself. "He's sitting with *them*!"

Aimee and Jordan were laughing. Cracking up, in fact. They looked as if they were having a blast. Well, well, well. Aimee was certainly enjoying Jordan's dumb jokes. If Sky and Sam and Alex couldn't see how Jordan was turning into a grade-A jerk right before their eyes, that was their problem. Not Carrie's. No . . . if Jordan wanted to act like a jock, fine. He would just have to suffer the consequences . . .

# M·a·k·i·n·g F·r·i·e·n·d·s

All *Making Friends* titles can be ordered at your local bookshop or are available by post from Book Service by Post (tel: 01624 675137).

# Making Friends

# Tough luck, Carrie

Kate Andrews

MACMILLAN CHILDREN'S BOOKS

First published 1998 by Macmillan Children's Books
a division of Macmillan Publishers Limited
25 Eccleston Place, London SW1W 9NF
and Basingstoke

Associated companies throughout the world

ISBN 0 330 35125 7

1 3 5 7 9 8 6 4 2

A CIP catalogue record for this book is available from
the British Library

Printed and bound in Great Britain by Mackays of Chatham plc, Kent

# The cast of
# M·a·k·i·n·g  F·r·i·e·n·d·s

## Alex

**Age:** 13

**Looks:** Light brown hair, blue eyes

**Family:** Mother died when she was a baby; lives with her dad and her brother Matt, aged 14

**Likes:** Skateboarding; her family and friends; wearing baggy T-shirts and jeans; being adventurous; letting her feelings show!

**Dislikes:** People who make fun of her skateboard, her brother or her dad; dressing smart or girly; anything to do with maths or science; dishonesty

## Carrie

**Age:** 13

**Looks:** Long dark hair – often dyed black! Hazel eyes

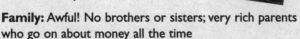

**Family:** Awful! No brothers or sisters; very rich parents who go on about money all the time

**Likes:** Writing stories; wearing black (drives her mum mad!); thinking deep thoughts; Sky's parents and their awesome houseboat!

**Dislikes:** Her full name – Carrington; her parents; her mum's choice of clothes; jokes about her hair; computers

# Sky

**Age:** 13

**Looks:** Light brown skin, dark hair, brown eyes

**Family:** Crazy! Lives on a houseboat with weird parents and a brother, Leif, aged 8

**Likes:** Shopping; trendy gear; TV; pop music; talking!

**Dislikes:** Her parents' bizarre lifestyle; having no money; eating meat

# Jordan

**Age:** 13

**Looks:** Floppy fair hair, green eyes

**Family:** Uncomfortable! Four big brothers – all so brilliant at sports he can never compete with them

**Likes:** Drawing! (especially cartoons); basketball (but don't tell anyone!); playing sax (badly); taking the mickey out of his brothers

**Dislikes:** Being "baby brother" to four brainless apes; Sky when she starts gossiping

# Sam

**Age:** 13

**Looks:** Native-American; very dark hair, very dark eyes

**Family:** Confusing! Both parents are Native-American but have different views on how their kids should look and behave; one sister – Shawna, aged 16

**Likes:** Skateboarding with Alex; computers (especially surfing the Net); writing for the school paper; goofing around

**Dislikes:** The way his friends dump their problems on each other; his parents' arguments

# Amy

**Age:** 13

**Looks:** Sickeningly gorgeous blonde hair; baby blue eyes (yuck!)

**Family:** Spoilt rotten by her dad, which worries her mum; two big sisters

**Likes:** Having loads of expensive clothes; making other people feel stupid; Matt (Alex's brother) – she fancies him; being leader of "The Amys" – her bunch of snobby friends

**Dislikes:** Alex, Carrie and Sky! Looking stupid or childish

# Mel

**Age:** 13

**Looks:** Black hair, dark eyes

**Family:** Nice parents who work very hard to do their best for Mel

**Likes:** Her mum and dad; her friends – but should these be the Amys, or Alex, Carrie and Sky? Standing up for herself; reading horror novels

**Dislikes:** Amy, when she's rotten to other people; worrying about who are her *real* friends

# One

*I know I'm going to end up at the mall this afternoon,* Carrie Mersel thought, slumping in her chair. She stared at a plate of lukewarm meat loaf, listening to Skyler Foley jabber on and on about some end-of-the-fall blowout sale. *Yup. I just know it.*

Carrie wasn't a huge fan of hanging out at the mall. As a matter of fact, she wasn't a huge fan of shopping, period. But Sky had that insane look in her big brown eyes. It was almost as if there were a glowing billboard inside her head flashing: Prices Slashed! 50% Off! Everything Must Go!

"You *have* to come with me," Sky was complaining to Alex Wagner. She twirled her long brown curls around her fingers. "You can skateboard in the parking lot."

Alex shot a glance across the round cafeteria table at Sam Wells. "Sky, I hate to tell you this, but skateboarding at the mall ... well ..."

1

"Stinks?" Sam finished for her, raising his black eyebrows.

Alex laughed. "To put it nicely." She reached into her baggy jeans' pocket and grabbed her wool hat, then pulled it over her tousled, shoulder-length dark blond hair. "Come on, Sky. The parking lot there is totally flat and boring. Even *you* know that. And you don't skate."

Sky shrugged. "So you'll just have to come shopping with me," she said brightly.

Carrie had to smile. Poor Sky. She could never bring herself to go to the mall alone. She always figured she might miss out on something. Sky *hated* missing out. So she usually ended up trying to convince everyone else to do whatever she was doing. Of course, more often than not, that meant going to the mall.

"Carrie—you'll come, right?" Sky pressed.

"Sure," Carrie replied grudgingly. She knew it was pointless to fight Sky on this. Besides, Sky *was* the only person on the planet who could actually make the mall semitolerable. She always knew exactly where Carrie could find really good cheap black hair dye. And cheap black shoes. And cheap black

2

dresses. Sky was the master bargain hunter.

"Well, personally *I* would *love* to join all of you in the wonderful world of shop-o-rama," Jordan Sullivan announced sarcastically as he used his fork to create a bizarre sculpture with his mashed potatoes. "But I can't."

Carrie rolled her eyes. She wondered for a moment how Jordan could even see what he was doing. His messy blond bangs practically hung to his nose.

"Why not?" Sky asked, smirking.

Jordan raised his head and brushed aside his hair. "Because I have basketball practice," he stated evenly.

Carrie hesitated, waiting for the punch line. Obviously this was some sort of goofy joke. She exchanged a quick, puzzled glance with Alex and Sam. But they looked just as confused as she did.

Jordan started grinning.

Finally Sky cleared her throat. "Uh . . . I hate to break it to you, Jor-*dumb*, but you aren't on the basketball team, remember?"

"Yeah, I am," he said in a perfectly natural voice. "I went to tryouts yesterday. They posted the roster outside Principal

3

Cashen's office this morning. You're looking at one of the Robert Lowell Panthers. It's official. You can check it out yourself."

Carrie frowned. Could he actually be telling the *truth?* No way. Jordan vowed long ago that he would never join any sports team. Joining a team meant following in the footsteps of his jock brothers. And as his best friend—or one of them, anyway—Carrie knew that Jordan would rather wear a bright pink polka-dot dress than do something his brothers would approve of.

"So what are you *really* doing?" Sky prodded, sounding impatient.

Jordan shrugged. "I told you."

Sam shook his head. His dark eyes narrowed. "Okay, man," he said, smiling dubiously. "Joke's over."

Jordan laughed again. "You guys—I'm *serious.*" He stopped sculpting the blob of mashed potatoes and looked Sam straight in the face. "Coach Powell told me I should give it a shot, so I did."

*He* is *serious,* Carrie suddenly realized. If he weren't, he wouldn't have been able to stare at Sam like that. He always avoided people's eyes when he was joking around.

"Look, I was going to tell you guys about it earlier," Jordan went on. "But it just never came up. Anyway—"

"You're really on the basketball team?" Carrie blurted.

He lifted his shoulders and smiled broadly. "Guilty as charged."

Carrie's brow grew furrowed. This was crazy. Everybody knew what kind of people played basketball at Robert Lowell Middle School—namely self-centered, stuck-up jerks. She just couldn't buy that Jordan wanted to be like *them*. "But *why?*" she demanded.

Jordan cocked an eyebrow. "Jeez," he mumbled jokingly. "You make it seem like I'm joining a motorcycle gang or something."

"It's *worse* than joining a motorcycle gang!" Carrie exclaimed. "It's . . . it's—"

"Hey, Jordan—you told me once that you would *never* join the team," Alex piped up. "Remember? You said you wanted to keep your hoop skills a secret from your family. Those were your exact words."

"I know." Jordan put down his fork and flashed her a cocky grin. "But Alex, when you got skills like mine, you *can't* keep them a secret."

Alex groaned. "Give me a break."

"I don't get it, though," Carrie said urgently, leaning forward and resting her elbows on the edge of the table. "What made you change your mind? I mean, I thought you wanted to avoid being like your brothers at all costs."

Jordan smiled crookedly. "Hey—just because I like playing hoops doesn't mean I'm gonna wind up like *them*. Not unless I get a brain transplant with a chimpanzee. Anyway, I would have joined the team last year if my brother hadn't been around. I just didn't want anybody to compare him to me. But now that Mark is gone, there's no reason to pretend that I don't play basketball anymore."

Carrie just shook her head. She was kind of annoyed, actually. This whole thing was so *un*-Jordan. It was almost as if he were selling out or something. Was he really going to waste his afternoons bouncing a dumb ball with meatheads like Johnny Bates and Chris Tanzell? When would he have time do all the other stuff he did—like draw cartoons? Or produce hideous screeching noises with his saxophone? Or hang out with his friends . . .

"So I guess we should congratulate you," Sky mumbled grudgingly. "Right?"

Jordan's smile widened. "I guess."

Sam nodded. "Definitely. Way to go, my man. I'm psyched to watch you go out there and kick some butt."

Carrie rolled her eyes.

"Or get your butt kicked," Alex teased. She quickly patted Jordan's shoulder. "Just kidding, pal."

"You probably won't see very much of either," Jordan admitted. "I won't be getting a lot of playing time. I mean, I'm not gonna be first-string or anything. . . ."

*If you aren't going to be first-string, then why did you even bother joining the team?* Carrie found herself wondering. Her gaze drifted through the big glass windows out to the courtyard. She caught a glimpse of a bunch of fifth and sixth graders with a basketball. They looked amazingly stupid. Jordan was giving up his free time for *that?*

"You can actually come watch me in three days," Jordan added. "Our first game is here on Friday, against Shepherd. You know, that school in Seattle? They beat us in the championship last year. They're our archrivals.

It'll be a great game." He glanced at Carrie. "What do you say? Will you be there?"

Carrie shrugged. "If I'm not going to the mall with Sky," she muttered.

"Oh, come on," Jordan protested with a good-natured smirk. "You guys can miss one day of shopping for this."

Sky shook her head. "I don't know, Jordan," she said matter-of-factly. "The sale *ends* on Friday."

Jordan glared at her. "Sky—"

"We'll be there," Carrie interrupted. "But will we get to see you play at all? I mean, if you're just going to be sitting on the bench . . ."

"Coach Powell always puts everyone on the team in at least once during a game," Jordan stated confidently. "Don't worry. You'll get to see me play."

Carrie forced herself to smile. But deep down she didn't really *want* to see Jordan play. Unless he wasn't going to play well. As mean as it made her feel, she wanted to see Jordan make a fool of himself on the court. That way he would get embarrassed. Then he would quit the team and give up basketball forever. Then everything would be back to normal. He'd *never* end up like his brothers. He wouldn't end up like the stuck-up jock dolts on the team, either.

He wouldn't change at all.

And that's what he really wanted, right?

# Two

"*Let's go, Panthers—let's go! Let's go, Panthers. . . .*"

Jordan swallowed. The gym was packed. It was louder than a rock concert in here. Who would have thought that the entire school would stay after classes to watch a lousy basketball game? Okay—so the Panthers *were* playing their archrivals. But still . . . didn't people have better things to do with their Friday afternoons?

"*Let's go, Panthers. . . .*"

He couldn't bring himself to turn and look at the bleachers. If he saw how many people were back there, he'd freak. He should have never opened his big mouth to his friends about this. Joining the team had been a huge mistake—

"Sullivan!" Coach Powell barked from the opposite end of the bench.

*Uh-oh.* Jordan's stomach lurched. He wasn't going to have to play *now*, was he?

The game was almost over. He'd deliberately sat at this end in hopes that Coach Powell would just forget about him. He couldn't go out there. Not in front of so many people. . . .

*"Sullivan!"* Coach Powell shouted. His voice sliced through the chanting crowd. "Get over here!"

Jordan nodded. Okay, okay. So he was going to play. No big deal. Just as long as he didn't pass out or yack all over the place, it would be fine, right? Chances were that nobody would even pass him the ball. He wiped his moist palms on his thighs and forced himself to march the length of the bench.

"How ya feelin', Sullivan?" Coach Powell demanded.

"Fine," Jordan lied. He *had* to say that. Coach Powell wasn't exactly the most understanding guy in the world. He sort of reminded Jordan of a talking fist. His face was really craggy and square and hairless. He had no neck, either. His head looked as if it had been jammed onto the top of his body. Jordan just hoped the old man couldn't see his knees wobbling.

"I'm gonna put you in for Tanzell."

Coach Powell grunted. "I would have put you in earlier, but I decided to save you. I didn't want Shepherd to know about your outside shot." His thick lips curled in a grin. "They're gonna be surprised."

Jordan managed a nod. *They are?* Was that what Coach Powell really thought? It was flattering—but the awful queasiness in Jordan's stomach was now about a million times worse. He glanced at the scoreboard.

*Oh no.*

The score was tied at thirty-eight points apiece. There were only twenty seconds left. That meant Coach Powell was putting the fate of the entire game in Jordan's hands.

"Time out, Robert Lowell," the referee called, blowing his whistle.

*"Let's go, Panthers!"* the crowd kept chanting—except now they were stamping their feet and clapping as well. *"Let's go, Panthers!"*

Jordan forced a weak smile as his teammates jogged off the court and huddled around Coach Powell. "Great game," he mumbled.

None of them smiled back. None of them even said anything. Then again, Jordan hadn't really expected them to respond. When Jordan had first made the team, he'd been psyched to make friends with the rest of the Panthers. But guys like Chris Tanzell and Johnny Bates had made it clear all week long that they thought Jordan was the biggest loser in the state of Washington.

"All right, guys, listen up," the coach announced. "We're gonna have a substitution. . . ."

*Why is he doing this to me?* Jordan wondered miserably. Nobody wanted him to play. Jordan didn't fit in with this team, plain and simple. He even *looked* different from the rest of his teammates. Everybody else looked as if they were related or something. They all had dark hair and mean eyes and muscles that would probably be normal on an eighteen-year-old. Not Jordan. He knew his pale arms and legs looked ridiculously scrawny in this baggy black uniform.

"You're putting *Sullivan* in for *me?*" Chris Tanzell cried. "But Coach—"

"No 'buts,' Tanzell," Coach Powell growled. "Take a seat."

For a moment Chris looked as if he were going to say something else. Then he snorted. After glaring at Jordan, he stormed to the end of the bench.

"Hey, Tanzell!" Coach Powell yelled after him. "I can do without the attitude, all right? There's no *i* in *team*, remember?"

Jordan hung his head. This was just perfect. Now his teammates hated him even more than they had before. He could just picture what they'd do to him if he missed this shot. They'd probably stuff him down one of the toilets in the boys' locker room.

"Okay, guys," Coach Powell stated. "Go do your thing."

*Right*, Jordan said to himself. *Do your thing. Translation: Make a fool of yourself.*

"Number twenty-three, Jordan Sullivan, is entering the game," a voice bellowed over the gym's loudspeaker. "He replaces Chris Tanzell."

*Oh, jeez.* Jordan gulped. But there was no turning back. The substitution was official now.

"You better not blow this, Sullivan," Johnny Bates hissed. "You'll regret it."

"Thanks a lot, man," Jordan muttered sarcastically. He wished he could either punch Johnny in the nose or bolt from the gym—or both. But as much as he hated to admit it, he knew Johnny was absolutely right.

If Jordan blew this shot, he'd be regretting it for a long, long time.

# Three

"Go, Jordan!" somebody yelled as Jordan walked out onto the court.

A cheer erupted from the crowd.

Jordan paused. Was that cheering for *him?* He summoned enough courage to look at the bleachers. Sure enough, Carrie, Sam, Alex, and Sky were on their feet, clapping and hollering for him—and everyone else in the stands had joined in.

"Go get 'em!" Sam shouted above the din.

A little half grin passed over Jordan's lips. *Wow.* Nobody had ever applauded for him before.

The whistle blew.

Jordan's knees buckled as the brief moment of confidence passed. Everyone on the basketball court scrambled to get into position.

Somebody passed the ball inbounds to Johnny.

*Okay*, Jordan thought, fighting back nausea and dizziness. *Just relax.*

Luckily he found himself being guarded by some little pipsqueak who came up to Jordan's chin. He couldn't help but smile. Shooting over this guy wouldn't be any problem. He felt a surge of hope. He just had to get open for the pass in time to make the shot.

The clock was ticking down. There were only fifteen seconds left.

"Move!" Coach Powell commanded from the sidelines.

Jordan faked to his left, then dashed to his right across the court—leaving the pipsqueak behind. Suddenly he was wide open. Johnny hurled the ball at him.

Jordan caught it and started dribbling. The pipsqueak was guarding him again, but Jordan could tell that the kid was tired— sweaty and out of breath. Not Jordan. Now that he was moving, he was pumped. More pumped than he'd ever been. Electric energy coursed through his veins.

All at once the crowd began counting down with the clock: *"Ten ... nine ... eight ..."*

Jordan's smiled widened. The ringing of

voices filled his ears. Any last traces of anxiety melted away. He *should* be freaking out right now. But he wasn't. He was right where he wanted to be—about fifteen feet from the basket. He'd made this exact same shot a thousand times in the driveway at Alex's house.

*"Five . . . four . . . three—"*

"Shoot it, you yutz!" Coach Powell shrieked.

Slowly, calmly, Jordan lifted the ball and let it fly from his fingertips—just over the outstretched hands of the pipsqueak. Silence filled the gym. The ball looked as if it were traveling in slow motion as it floated through the air . . . then plopped into the basket with a *swish*.

The buzzer sounded.

The entire gym exploded with a single word: *"Yesss!"*

Jordan's eyes bulged. The next thing he knew, he found himself being mauled by his teammates. . . . People were crowding around him, patting him on the back, shouting. . . . But he was in a complete daze. He'd known he could make the shot, but still . . .

17

"Way to go, man!" Johnny Bates cried, clapping him on the shoulder.

"Nice one, Sullivan!" Chris Tanzell called, giving him a thumbs-up.

In the all the shock and chaos Jordan just grinned. He couldn't think of a word to say. Gradually he became aware of a chant from the stands: "*Sul-li-van, Sul-li-van, Sul-li-van . . .*"

Wait a second. The entire gym was shouting his name. He started laughing. This was wild. *His* name.

He'd done it.

He'd *won* the game for Robert Lowell.

People started pouring out of the bleachers and onto the gym floor. Jordan hopped up on his tiptoes, scanning the sea of faces for Carrie and the others. . . .

"Jordan?" a girl's voice asked from behind him.

Jordan whirled around. He found himself face-to-face with . . . *Aimee Stewart?*

She'd never even talked to him before. But why would she? She was one of the Amys—one of the three most popular, coolest, best-looking girls at Robert Lowell. The Amys didn't have time for guys like Jordan. He paused, half expecting her to ask him to get out of the way or something. But she didn't. She stood right in front of him, smiling shyly, her blue eyes glittering under her blond curls.

"I just wanted to congratulate you," she said over the noise. "That was an awesome shot."

Jordan's jaw dropped. *Congratulate me?* His heart pounded. "Uh . . . thanks," he finally mumbled.

"I want to talk to you about it later," she went on. "I'm going to write an article about it in the school paper."

"Schoo-school paper?" Jordan stuttered, totally overwhelmed. She laughed once. "Is that okay?"

"Yeah!" he exclaimed. "I mean . . . sure."

"Good. I'll give you a call later."

Jordan just nodded, unable to keep from staring into her eyes. He couldn't believe it. Aimee Stewart was going to write about him. Not Chris Tanzell, not Johnny Bates—but *him.*

He realized something at that moment.

He should have joined the basketball team a *long* time ago.

\*     \*     \*

"Jordan!" Carrie yelled, struggling to climb down the bleachers onto the crowded gym floor with Alex, Sky, and Sam trailing behind her. She couldn't believe that Jordan had won the game. It was awesome. Well, not *that* awesome. She didn't want him to get full of himself or anything. But she *was* proud of him. Now if she could only make it through all these screaming people, then she could actually congratulate him for making the shot. . . .

"Jordan!" Alex shouted from behind her.

He was barely twenty feet away, in the middle of all the commotion, grinning and trying to answer a million questions at once. But he didn't even so much as glance in their direction. Nope. For some bizarre reason his eyes seemed to be glued to Aimee Stewart.

*"Jordan!"* Carrie called a second time.

For a split second his gaze seemed to flicker up into the stands. But then he turned right back to Aimee, as if his head were being yanked with an invisible string.

Carrie abruptly stopped.

"Jordan!" Alex shouted again breathlessly. "Over here!"

But Jordan just kept staring at Aimee. Carrie frowned. What was his problem? Why was he ignoring them?

Before Carrie could open her mouth again, the mob surrounding Jordan suddenly began to move. Once again people started chanting: *"Sul-li-van, Sul-li-van, Sul-li-van . . ."*

Carrie slowly folded her arms across her chest. Now *this* was absurd. Jordan didn't even know those people.

She couldn't believe it. Jordan Sullivan—*her* friend—was being treated like a full-fledged jock. Not only that, he was *acting* like one, too. He was wearing the same slimy, self-satisfied look on his face that all jocks wore. Yup, Carrie knew the look well. She saw it every single day on the faces of guys like Chris Tanzell and Johnny Bates.

*He's becoming just like them*, Carrie said to herself grimly. She shook her head as the crowd swept out of the gym, looking like some kind of giant alien creature with dozens of heads and arms and legs. *One*

21

*lousy shot, and he's becoming just like them.*

She was *not* prepared to let that happen.

Carrie nodded, feeling as if she had a mission.

Yes, sir. She was going to have a little chat with Robert Lowell's newest hero. She was going to give him a piece of her mind. And after that, Jordan would think twice about letting his ego get in the way of his friends again.

# Four

Carrie stood at the end of her driveway on Monday morning, waiting for the bus to pick her up. A light drizzle was falling. Unfortunately she didn't own a raincoat. Well, she *did* own a hideous yellow thing that made her look like a bumblebee. But she would never wear that in a billion years. Besides, she could care less about foul weather right now. She had more important things on her mind.

She still had to figure out what she was going to say to Jordan.

Maybe she would let *him* do the talking at first. Yeah. She would give him a chance to apologize for blowing her off on Friday. He deserved that much. After all, everyone had swarmed on him after the game like he was some kind of NBA superstar or something. He obviously didn't know how to deal with all that attention. So in a way his behavior was forgivable. Lame, but forgivable. Now he'd had the entire weekend to think about what a jerk he'd been—so he would say that he was sorry. Naturally.

*Then* she would congratulate him.

And she would definitely not overreact, either. Nope. After all, he'd only played for about twenty seconds.

She shook her head. This was so stupid. If he'd only messed up like he was supposed to, then she wouldn't have to think about what she was going to say. . . .

Bus number four swerved around the corner onto Whidbey Road. It jerked to a stop in a huge puddle at the end of the driveway—instantly soaking Carrie's black dress, her socks, and her combat boots.

Carrie frowned. How nice.

Brick, the bus driver, opened the door. "Sorry, Carrie," he croaked. His eyes were puffy, as if he hadn't slept in days. Of course, knowing Brick, he probably hadn't. He was quite the partier. "I didn't mean to get you wet."

"That's okay, Brick," Carrie mumbled, sighing. She lumbered up the steps.

"That's the great thing about black. It looks just as good wet as it does dry."

His haggard face brightened. "Hey, you're right!" he exclaimed. "I never noticed that!"

Carrie had to smile. What a guy. Brick had a brain the size of a pea and a heart the size of a watermelon. She turned down the aisle. "Maybe I should hose myself down every day—" Suddenly she froze.

*What the . . .*

Jordan was sitting in the first seat.

With Amy Anderson.

But that wasn't all. He was draped over the back of the seat, chatting it up with Aimee Stewart and Mel Eng, who were sitting behind him. They looked as if they were all lifelong buddies or something. Carrie's mouth hung open. For a second she literally felt as if she were witnessing a scene in one of her own horror stories. What on *earth* was going on here? *Nobody* ever sat with the Amys. Least of all her best friend . . .

"Did you go for a swim this morning?" Amy Anderson asked Carrie dryly, glancing at her sopping dress.

A few kids on the other side of the aisle giggled. But for once Carrie was *way* too freaked to acknowledge some lame wisecrack.

"Jordan?" she gasped.

He glanced up at her. "Hey!" he cried enthusiastically. He smiled as if absolutely nothing were wrong. "Guess what? I'm getting interviewed for the school paper. Aimee says it's going to be on the front page."

Carrie could only gape at him, horrified.

"Hey, Carrie?" Brick murmured. "You gotta have a seat."

Carrie shifted her stunned eyes to Mel and Aimee. Both of them were scowling. Their expressions clearly stated: *Beat it*.

Fine. Carrie shook her head—then stormed down the aisle to the backseat, where Alex and Sam were waiting. She slumped between them, folding her arms across her chest.

The bus bounced forward.

"I don't believe it," she grumbled, staring at the rain-splattered floor. "What's gotten into him? What does he think he's *doing*?"

"He's getting interviewed for the paper," Sam offered cautiously.

26

"So I heard," Carrie growled. She glanced up for a moment. Once again Jordan was yammering away happily, staring into the eyes of Aimee Stewart. It was completely disgusting. "'Aimee says it's going to be on the front page,'" she mocked in a high-pitched voice.

Alex laughed once. "What's the matter? Don't you think it's cool?"

"*Cool?*" Carrie cried. She turned and looked Alex straight in the face. "He's sitting up there with the Amys instead of back here where he belongs—and you think it's *cool?*"

Alex lowered her eyes. She reached for her damp brown wool cap and began to fidget with it. "I just think it's cool that there's gonna be an article about Jordan in the *Robert Lowell Observer*," she mumbled. "That's all I meant."

"Article, huh?" Carrie muttered. She shifted her gaze back to Jordan. Rage burned inside her. "I'll show him an article. . . ."

*Hold on.*

A wicked smile spread across Carrie's face.

Of course. She *would* show Jordan an article. She'd show everyone else at Robert Lowell an article, too. Aimee could write her dumb piece—but Carrie would write one, too. She would write an editorial. The Amys might have control of the newspaper, but they had no say over the editorials. Those went straight through Principal Cashen.

So if Carrie wrote a brilliant editorial that made fools out of all the incredibly stupid, conceited, and arrogant jocks at Robert Lowell . . . well, then Principal Cashen would be sure to print it. Even better, Jordan Sullivan would be sure to read it.

Ha!

And how would Robert Lowell's newest basketball star feel after *that*?

# Five

## I

By the time Carrie slumped down beside Alex at the lunch table, her editorial was nearly finished. But she was starting to have second thoughts about turning it in. It was pretty harsh. *Really* harsh, actually. She'd spent all morning in a total frenzy, writing the piece during her classes instead of listening or taking notes. Maybe she'd let her anger get the best of her. Besides, it was pretty clear that Alex, Sam, and Sky didn't think that Jordan had done anything wrong by sitting with the Amys on the bus that morning.

"Isn't it awesome about Jordan?" Alex suddenly asked, as if reading Carrie's mind. "Everybody's been talking about him all day. He's become like a ... like a ..." She snapped her fingers, searching for the right word.

"Jerk?" Carrie suggested dryly.

Alex smirked. "No, Carrie. I was

thinking more along the lines of like . . . like *legend* or something."

"Legend?" Carrie snorted. "Yeah—in his own mind."

"Oh, come on." Alex laughed. "You have to admit, this is a pretty big deal. . . ." Her voice trailed off as Sam and Sky sat down at the table.

"What's up?" Sam asked. "What are you guys talking about?"

"What else?" Carrie grumbled. "Robert Lowell's latest sports sensation."

Sam grinned at Carrie. "You aren't still mad about what happened on the bus, are you?"

Carrie bit her lip. Of course she was still mad. But nobody here knew just how mad. She hadn't told anyone about her editorial yet.

"Well, I think it's great that Aimee Stewart is writing an article about Jordan," Sam said quietly.

*"What?"* Carrie yelled.

Sam shrugged. "Hey, I'm not saying I *like* her. I'm just saying that a lot of people listen to what she says. Like ninety-nine percent of the school. And if she says good things about Jordan, well . . . then that's a good thing. Right?"

Carrie just grunted. Okay. So she kind of saw Sam's point. But that didn't excuse the fact that Jordan had totally blown Carrie off at the basketball game. Now that he thought he was some kind of jock, he was just psyched to hang out with the "in" crowd. And obviously Aimee didn't *like* him. No . . . she just wanted to use him for a good story—then toss him aside like a discarded chicken bone as soon as he quit the team.

And he *would* quit the team. Carrie was sure he'd come to his senses sooner or later.

Well . . . unless, of course, he really *was* becoming a jock.

## II

"Hey, Jordan!" a familiar girl's voice called.

Jordan paused in the crowded cafeteria, clutching his lunch tray. For a second he couldn't tell where the voice was coming from. It definitely *wasn't* coming from his usual table. No, Carrie, Alex, Sky, and Sam were all sitting there, staring at him blankly. So where? It was way too noisy in here.

"Over here!" the girl called again, laughing.

Jordan pivoted on his feet—turning, turning . . .

*Aimee?*

Aimee Stewart was standing by the Amys' table, waving. At *him*. In front of the entire cafeteria. He blinked twice. It didn't make any sense.

"Come sit with us!" she yelled, pointing toward an empty chair beside her. "We have to finish the interview!"

Jordan stared at her. Okay. On the one hand, it was very bizarre that Aimee was paying so much attention to him. . . . But on the other hand, why fight it? He smiled. Now that he got a good look at Aimee, he noticed that her green dress was actually pretty cute. Funny. He never thought about things like that. Well, almost never. He took a few steps forward, then slowed.

Amy and Mel were sitting at the table, too—whispering to each other.

*Hmmm.* Something about the way they kept glancing up at him and smiling made him uneasy. Then again, Amy and Mel were the kind of girls who were always whispering about *something*. And they had been totally cool to him on the bus.

"Come *on*," Aimee urged. She patted the chair next to her.

Nah—there was nothing to worry about. Anyway, this was kind of a dream come true, wasn't it? He was being asked to sit with the Amys. Every guy at Robert Lowell would kill for this opportunity. Without another moment's hesitation he strode across the cafeteria and sat down beside Aimee.

### III

"Do—do—do you *see* that?" Carrie sputtered. She jerked a trembling finger across the cafeteria at the back of Jordan's head, unable to control herself. "He's sitting with *them!*"

Sky shrugged. "You heard Aimee," she said calmly, digging into a plastic container of homemade salad. "She wants to finish the interview."

"So what?" Carrie hissed. Suddenly she realized she was grinding her teeth. But she couldn't help it. She was seething.

33

"This is the *second* time today Jordan dissed us for the Amys. We *always* sit together at lunch." Her voice rose. "It's like, now that he's a jock, he feels like he has to hang out with Amys because *all* the jocks hang out with the Amys, like Chris Tanzell and Johnny—"

"Uh, Carrie?" Sky interrupted, peering at her nervously. "You sure about all that?"

Carrie frowned. "Of *course* I'm sure."

Sky raised her eyebrows, then went back to eating her salad. "Okay," she mumbled with her mouth full. "I'm just saying that there's a slight chance Aimee actually wants to finish the interview."

"Since when do *you* stick up for Aimee Stewart?" Carrie cried.

"I'm not sticking up for her." Sky shook her head. "Jeez. I thought *I* was the paranoid one. Listen, just be thankful that we don't have to listen to any of Jordan's dumb jokes today," she added with a smile.

Carrie didn't say anything more. Her eyes wandered back to Jordan's table. Aimee and Jordan were laughing. Cracking up, in fact. They looked as if they were having a blast. Well, well, well. *Aimee* was certainly enjoying Jordan's dumb jokes. If Sky and Sam and Alex couldn't see how Jordan was turning into a grade-A jerk right before their very eyes, that was *their* problem. Not Carrie's. No . . . any last doubts about turning in that editorial were fading fast. If Jordan wanted to act like a jock, fine. He would just have to suffer the consequences.

## IV

Jordan leaned back in his chair, unable to believe how *relaxed* he felt. Maybe he'd been expecting to be really intimidated or something. But eating lunch with Aimee, Mel, and Amy seemed as natural as . . . well, eating lunch with his friends. It was weird: Carrie and Alex and Sky were totally wrong about the Amys. As a matter of fact, he was actually beginning to understand why the Amys were the most popular kids at Robert Lowell. They didn't just *act* really cool. They *were* really cool.

"So what made you wait so long to join the basketball team?" Aimee asked, leaning toward him. "I mean, you're obviously really good. You should have started playing in sixth grade. We would have won the championship by now."

Jordan could feel his face getting hot. *Oh, brother*. He didn't want to start blushing right now and making a complete fool out of himself. "Well, uh . . . to tell you the truth, I just didn't want to play on the same team as my brother Mark," he said quickly. He laughed once. "I mean, I don't know if you ever noticed, but I don't exactly get along with him."

"Why not?" Amy Anderson piped up. She exchanged a quick glance with Mel. The two of them giggled. "He seems fine to me. *Very* fine."

Jordan fought back the urge to sneer. *Fine?* He could think of another word. Okay . . . so maybe the Amys weren't all *that* cool. Aimee was definitely much cooler than the other two. Then again, he'd always known that Amy Anderson was in love with Mark. Of course, Amy also had a crush on Alex's older brother. She probably had a crush on every guy over the age of fourteen in the greater Seattle area.

"I just didn't want to embarrass him on

the court," Jordan finally mumbled. "It's tough when your younger brother can kick your butt, you know?" He flashed Amy a brief, phony smile. "I'm a sensitive kind of guy."

Amy just snickered. So did Mel.

But Aimee threw back her head and hooted with laughter. "Sensitive guy!" she cried. "Jordan—you're so *funny!*"

Jordan jumped slightly. *Wow.* None of his friends had ever told him that. In fact, they always groaned at his jokes. He *knew* he was blushing now.

Amy exchanged another quick glance with Mel.

"So now that he's gone, there's nothing holding you back, right?" Aimee asked once she'd gotten a grip on herself.

Jordan shrugged. "I guess not."

Aimee leaned closer. Her eyes bored into Jordan's own. "I'm glad," she murmured. "It looks to me like the Sullivan family saved its best for last."

## V

Carrie squirmed in her seat, drumming her shiny black fingernails loudly on the table. If Aimee and Jordan sat any closer, they'd practically be *touching*. This was supposed to be an interview? Yeah, right. It looked more like a really cheesy teen romance movie. Things had gone too far. Way too far. What was Jordan *thinking* right now?

"Um . . . Carrie?" Alex said.

"What?" Carrie asked shortly, keeping her gaze riveted to Jordan.

"Are you all right?"

"Fine," Carrie stated.

"Uh . . . maybe we should all go outside," Sam suggested. "We can start recess a little early today. It's not raining anymore. . . ."

But Carrie had stopped listening. She held her breath. Aimee was draping her hand over the back of Jordan's chair. Carrie started shaking her head. Her stomach tightened. This couldn't be happening. Acting like a jock was one thing . . . but this, *this* was insane.

"Look!" Carrie hissed, pointing. "Look at that!" Her eyes darted wildly around at her friends' faces. "Aimee is, like, putting her arm around Jordan!"

Nobody said a word.

"Look!" Carrie repeated, a little desperately.

Slowly everyone at the table turned toward Jordan. . . .

"Eww!" Sky cried, wrinkling her nose. "You're *right!*"

Sam started laughing. "Jordan, you devil!"

Carrie's eyes smoldered. She didn't think she'd ever *been* so angry. For a moment, as she glared at Jordan, she almost felt as if she were looking at a complete stranger. She didn't even *know* Jordan anymore. The Jordan Sullivan *she* knew would never have gotten so warm and cozy with one of the three wicked witches of Robert Lowell.

She did know one thing, though.

Her editorial wasn't nearly harsh *enough.* Nope. Without another word she jumped up from the table and stomped out of the cafeteria. She had some business to take care of before recess started.

**Jordan Sullivan: Robert Lowell's
Newest B-ball Sensation**

# Six

Jordan felt perfectly loose when he strolled out onto the empty gym floor for practice Wednesday afternoon. He was still reeling from Aimee's article. Nobody had ever been that complimentary about him. *Nobody.* Of course, the self-portrait he'd drawn had helped a lot. He grinned. It had taken up most of the entire front page. But hey—maybe he deserved all this hoopla for once in his life, right? He *had* made the game-winning shot on Friday.

He shook his head, then picked up a ball and started dribbling. His life had changed more since Friday than it had in the past three years at Robert Lowell. Instead of being ignored by the Amys, he was practically best friends with one of them. Johnny Bates and Chris Tanzell weren't pushing him around anymore. Everywhere he went, people smiled at him, waved at him, asked him for advice....

"Hey, Sullivan!" Chris Tanzell called from inside the locker room. "How does it feel to be a victim of your own stereotype?"

Jordan stopped dribbling. *A victim of my own stereotype?* What the . . .

"No, no—you got it wrong." Johnny Bates hooted. "The question is: How does it feel to be an egotistical snob?"

*Egotistical snob?* Jordan frowned. All right. Something very bizarre was happening. Either Johnny and Chris had each gained about forty IQ points in the last five minutes, or Jordan was losing his mind. Johnny probably didn't even know what a word like *egotistical* meant. He had trouble with any word over two syllables.

"What's going on in here?" Jordan demanded, dropping the ball and marching through the locker-room door. "What—"

He stopped in midsentence. The entire team was huddled around Johnny, laughing hysterically. He sat on one of the locker-room benches under a pale yellow fluorescent light, holding up a school newspaper for everyone to see.

Jordan pursed his lips. "What's so funny?"

"Come on, man," Chris muttered. "You

have to admit, this is pretty good."

"*What's* good?" Jordan demanded. "What are you talking about?"

"What do you *think* we're talking about?" Johnny groaned. "Your friend's letter, dummy."

"Letter?" Jordan repeated uneasily. "What letter?"

Johnny glanced up. "What—are you saying you haven't seen the editorial page?"

Suddenly Jordan realized that everyone in the room was staring at him. He shook his head. "No," he croaked.

There was a pause.

The next thing Jordan knew, everybody started cracking up again.

"Oh, man," Johnny mumbled, shaking his head. He pushed himself to his feet and handed Jordan the paper—pointing to an editorial. "I'm sorry, dude. Really. I thought you knew."

Almost instantly Jordan's eyes zeroed in on the name at the bottom of the letter. *Carrie Mersel.* He swallowed. Carrie had written a letter? Why hadn't she told him? What *was* this? Holding his breath, he began to devour the words.

To Whom It May Concern:

Recently some disturbing events at our school have caused me to do a lot of thinking about two four-letter words: *jock* and *hype*.

As everyone knows, jocks are the coolest of the cool. They're good-looking and popular—and they never let the rest of us forget it.

Nevertheless, I've always maintained that a good athlete doesn't have to be good-looking, popular, or full of himself. But once you get labeled as a jock, the label tends to stick. That's when the trouble begins. That's when you start thinking that you're better, cooler, and more popular than everyone else.

Take the case of a certain basketball star. I know this star very well. He doesn't possess any of those stereotypically "jock" traits. Not a single one.

Or at least he *didn't*. Not until after he won a game.

This leads me to the second word: *hype*. Sadly, this star came to believe his own hype. Now he thinks he *is* a jock. Moreover, he thinks that being a jock is a good thing to be. After all, jocks are cool, right? Being an egotistical snob is fine as long as you can put a ball through a hoop.

Perhaps it sounds as if I'm being harsh. But as a school we have to recognize our own power. We labeled this player as a jock. Days later he tried to become one. He became a victim of his own stereotype. We have to think twice before labeling people.

Thoughtfully yours,
Carrie Mersel

"I do—I do-don't *believe* it!" Jordan stammered. "This is *sick!*"

Johnny just kept laughing. "I told you, man."

Without thinking, Jordan crumpled the paper in his hands and hurled it to the floor—then bolted from the locker room. He had to talk to Carrie. *Now.* She'd obviously suffered some kind of complete mental breakdown. . . . Hopefully bus number four hadn't left yet. Jordan burst through the gym doors, nearly slamming into Coach Powell.

"Sullivan!" Coach Powell barked. "Where do you think you're going?"

"Can't talk!" Jordan gasped, sprinting down the hall toward the front of the school. "I'll be right back."

Ready to explode, Jordan picked up his pace. How could Carrie *do* this to him? He shoved through the crowd of kids at the front door and leaped down the concrete steps. Brick was just closing the bus door.

*"Wait!"* Jordan yelled.

The door squeaked open again.

Jordan stomped up the stairs.

"Hey, man!" Brick said cheerfully. "I thought you had practice—"

*"You!"* Jordan shouted, pointing down

the aisle at Carrie— who was sandwiched in the backseat between Alex and Sam. "Why did you do it? Why?"

Carrie started shaking her head. Her face was pale. "I . . . I . . ."

"Uh, Jordan?" Brick said, clearing his throat. "Are you gonna ride with us?" He chuckled nervously. "Because if you aren't, I'm gonna have to ask you to get off."

Jordan drew in a deep, quivering breath and nodded. "I'll get off," he panted. His heart sounded as if it were in the middle of some crazed thrash-metal drum solo. Yet even in his exhausted, frenzied state, he was able to make a decision. He had no idea *why* Carrie had flipped—but if she wanted a war, fine. She'd made the first move. Now it was his turn.

"Jordan?" Brick prodded.

Finally Jordan's breathing evened. "Sorry to hold you up," he said. He fixed Carrie with a calm gaze. "I just want to say one thing. I want to make one announcement. In front of this whole bus. As of right now Jordan Sullivan—the egotistical jock—is never talking to Carrie Mersel again. Ever."

And with that he marched back down the stairs and stalked off toward the gym.

# Seven

Carrie paced back and forth across the tiny back deck of Sky's houseboat. She couldn't keep still. She'd been pacing for the past twenty minutes. Alex, Sky, and Sam just stood there, leaning against the rail and staring at her as if she were a complete lunatic. They'd barely said a word since Jordan's little outburst on the bus. Of course, Carrie couldn't blame them. They were probably still in a state of shock. They'd found out about the editorial at the same time as the rest of the school.

"Hey, Carrie?" Sky asked quietly, twirling her brown hair around her fingers. "Maybe we should go inside. I think it might start raining again."

Carrie paused for a second and glanced up at the gray skies. Sky had a point. The wind had picked up. Big, black storm clouds were rolling in from the west over the Puget Sound horizon. But Carrie was way too agitated to be cooped up in the little cabin right now.

"In a minute," she mumbled.

Sky sighed. "Look, Carrie—I have to ask you. . . . What were you thinking? Why *did* you write that letter?"

"Why *wouldn't* I?" Carrie grumbled. She started pacing again. "I mean, Jordan has totally changed. He's turned into a jock. There's no denying it. First he blows us off after the game on Friday—"

"He didn't blow us off, Carrie," Sam interrupted quietly. "Every single person in the gym was crowding around him at once. There was no *way* we could have talked to him."

Carrie shook her head. "But I was yelling his name!" she insisted.

"He didn't hear you," Alex murmured, lowering her eyes. She took off her wool cap and began fiddling with it. A powerful breeze blew a few wisps of dark blond hair across her face. "I was yelling his name, too, remember? He swears he didn't hear us. I asked him about it this morning. He was *looking* for us." She lifted her head and

48

met Carrie's gaze. "But he couldn't even see anything. All those people were jumping around and shouting in his ear."

Carrie opened her mouth for a second, then shut it. So maybe Alex and Sam were right. Maybe Jordan hadn't seen or heard them even though they'd been screaming their lungs out. Maybe, just *maybe*, Jordan hadn't purposely blown them off. But that still didn't excuse the fact that he'd sat on the bus with Aimee. Or that he'd eaten lunch with her. It didn't excuse the invisible magnet that seemed to be constantly pulling Jordan toward Robert Lowell's Most Heinous Creature—and *away* from his friends.

"What were you going to say?" Sky prodded.

"Nothing," Carrie mumbled. She turned to face the oncoming storm. Her long black dress billowed in the wind. "It's just . . . that he's not acting like himself. What about the way he's been hanging out with Aimee Stewart? I mean, he's spending every single free second with her. First the bus, then lunch. And then he's got practice after school." She glanced at the others. "When are *we* supposed to hang out with him?"

"Carrie—the only reason he was hanging out with Aimee so much was because of the article," Sam pleaded. "Come on. You *know* Jordan. Do you think he'd really eat lunch with the Amys every single day?"

"That's the whole point!" Carrie countered, throwing her hands in the air. "I don't even know anymore! I *don't* know Jordan. At least I don't feel like I do."

Sam sighed. "Well, I still know him," he stated. "I spoke to him on the phone last night. He was psyched to hang out with all of us this weekend. He said so."

Carrie's hands fell to her sides. "He did?"

"Yup." Sam nodded. "He *was* psyched, that is. But now . . . I mean, after what you wrote . . ." Sam's voice trailed off.

"Um—what did he say, exactly?" Carrie asked, swallowing. Her throat was dry. All at once her anger seemed to be melting away. Now she only felt a vague sort of nervousness.

Sam shrugged. "Just the norm. He wanted to go to this novelty shop in Seattle to load up on stink bombs for this prank he's pulling on his brothers. Believe me, Carrie—he's the same guy he always was." He shook his head and laughed sadly. "The only difference is that he's really, really mad right now."

Carrie blinked. Her stomach squeezed. Jordan wanted to get his brothers with stink bombs? That certainly sounded like the same old Jordan. Maybe Sam was right. Maybe her letter had been a little over the top. Maybe she should have tried to talk to Jordan again before handing it in. . . . *Oh, man.* She shook her head. A terrible feeling was creeping over her—the feeling she always got whenever she made a huge and incredibly dumb mistake. She knew it well. Yup. She had already felt it about a million times in the past year alone. . . .

"Hey, Carrie—are you all right?" Sky asked.

Carrie's head drooped. "Not really," she moaned. She glanced up at Sam. "Why didn't you tell me about this earlier?"

"Because I didn't think it mattered all that much," Sam replied in a matter-of-fact tone. "I mean—how was I supposed to know you were going to write a letter to the paper?"

Carrie nodded. "You're right, you're right," she mumbled dismally. "I'm sorry. It's not your fault at all. I just wish there was something I could do to take that letter back. . . ."

"Maybe there is," Sky suggested.

Carrie raised her eyebrows. "Like what?"

"Like going to Sheridan School in Seattle to watch Jordan play basketball tomorrow," Sky said.

Carrie groaned. "That's not even funny, Sky."

"No—just listen," Sky went on. "It'll be the perfect way for you guys to make up. See, the four of us will probably be the only Robert Lowell fans at the game. And once Jordan looks up in the stands and sees that you went all that way just to watch him play, he'll be totally flattered, and . . . and then everything will be back to normal." She took a deep breath. "Right?"

Carrie shook her head. "Wrong," she answered quietly. Another gust of wind sent a shiver down her spine. She wrapped her arms around herself and stared out at the gray, choppy waters of the Sound. "I mean, no offense—but it's gonna take a lot more than watching a lousy game to patch things up. You read the letter. I don't know. I guess I should apologize first."

"Probably. But the game's worth a shot, too. Isn't it?" Alex put in. "Really. Maybe you should give basketball a chance, you know what I mean?"

Carrie dubiously cocked her eyebrow at Alex. "Give basketball a chance?"

Alex nodded. "Yeah. It's like, I used to be totally bored by basketball until Matt got into it. Maybe the same thing will happen to you."

Carrie had to laugh. "Yeah," she said dryly. "And maybe I'll win the Miss Teen USA pageant next year."

Sam chuckled. "Hey—stranger things have happened, right? I agree with Sky and Alex."

Carrie gazed at the three of them for a moment. "You *really* think that going to this basketball game will help?" she finally asked.

Sky lifted her shoulders. "Look at it this way, Carrie," she said gently. "At this point you have absolutely nothing to lose. You *have* to clear the air with Jordan."

Carrie nodded. Sky was right. The way things were going, it looked as if she'd already lost her best friend. Why didn't she ever *think* before doing something so ridiculous? Why was she always letting herself get so riled up? But even as these questions raced through her mind, she knew there was no point in asking them. The damage had been done. And if becoming a basketball fan would mean getting Jordan back as a friend . . . well, then Carrie Mersel would become the biggest basketball fan on the planet.

Later that evening Carrie stared at the old-fashioned phone in her room, trying to get up the guts to call Jordan. She knew that her friends thought if Carrie showed up at the game, it would fix everything, but Carrie wasn't so sure. And she didn't think she could handle waiting all the way until tomorrow afternoon to find out.

"Oh, stop being such a wuss," she told

herself. Before she could change her mind, she reached over, grabbed up the receiver, and dialed Jordan's number.

He answered on the first ring.

"Hello?"

Carrie's heart was in her throat.

"Jordan, it's Carrie. Don't hang up," she said quickly.

There was a short sigh. "I told you I don't want to talk to you anymore. Or am I such a stupid jock, I didn't get my point across?"

Carrie took in a sharp breath. She supposed she deserved that.

"Look, Jordan, I'm sorry I wrote that letter before talking to you," she began, waiting to hear the click of the line being cut off. Thankfully it wasn't. "I just freaked because you were hanging with the Amys and those morons on the team—"

"Carrie, they're not morons. And I *like* playing on the team," Jordan said severely. "And you'd see that the Amys are pretty cool if you'd give them a chance." He paused. Carrie chewed her lip. "You know what your problem is, Carrie?"

"My problem?" Carrie wasn't aware that she had a problem. She'd made one mistake. What was the monster trauma?

"Your problem is that you can't deal with change," Jordan said. "I decided that I wanted to try something new—something that—yes—forces me to hang around with different people—and you blow it all out of proportion. Just because you refuse to ever wear color or come out of the Ice Age and use a computer doesn't mean the rest of us have to live in a cave."

Carrie's mouth dropped open. Afraid of change? Living in a cave? Was that what he really thought of her? So she liked what she liked. Was that so wrong?

"Jordan, I . . ." Carrie trailed off. She had no idea what to say. She didn't even know what to *think.*

"I gotta go, Carrie," Jordan said, sounding tired. "I'll see ya."

The line went dead in Carrie's ear.

Afraid of change? Ha! *Well, I'll show him!* Carrie thought as she slammed down the phone, stood up, and paced around her room. She was going to go to that game with her friends tomorrow. She was going to show Jordan that she was capable of trying new things—of traveling all the way to Seattle on a smelly old bus so she could try something new. And she was going to show him that she could enjoy basketball—even if it killed her.

# Eight

*This is the most depressing thing I've ever seen*, Carrie thought miserably, staring down at the basketball court.

Going to Jordan's first game had been halfway decent. At least Carrie didn't have to actually *go* anywhere—except the gym. But the bus ride to Sheridan School in Seattle had taken over an hour. And Sheridan's gym was totally . . . *dead*. It was like a cemetery in here or something. The only other people in the bleachers besides Carrie, Sky, Alex, and Sam were two tired-looking women who were obviously bored out of their skulls. One of them was actually knitting.

"Boy, they really pack 'em in here, don't they?" Sam whispered jokingly.

Carrie shook her head. "Maybe there's a reason nobody's here," she mumbled, glancing around at the rows and rows of empty seats. "Maybe Sheridan doesn't like to have people watch their games. Maybe we should just turn around and—"

"Don't even try it," Alex interrupted. She leaned forward in her seat and stared intently at Jordan and the other players. "We're here. Besides, the game has just started. As soon as we start making some noise, the energy is going to pick up. Trust me." She cupped her hands around her mouth. "Let's go, Panthers!" she shrieked.

"Let's go, Panthers!" Sky immediately joined in. "Let's go . . ."

*Oh, jeez.* Carrie winced. Yelling at a game where everyone else was yelling was one thing—but cheering wildly in a silent, deserted gym was just plain weird. Carrie looked back onto the court. Jordan was dribbling the ball, but his eyes kept darting up to the bleachers. He looked just as baffled as Carrie. She buried her face in her hands. Great. Jordan probably thought they had come here to make fun of him or something. There was no *way* this was going to help.

"All right, Jordan!" Alex suddenly yelled, leaping up. "Awesome shot!"

Carrie peered out from behind her fingers. Her eyes widened. *Wait a second.*

Jordan was suddenly *smiling* at them. He must have scored—because Chris Tanzell and Johnny Bates and some other guys were giving him high fives. He flashed a brief thumbs-up at Alex, then scurried back down the court. Carrie's lips twisted in a little grin. The change in Jordan's face was incredible. His green eyes were bright, his cheeks were rosy red, and his hair was flying all over the place. He actually looked as if he was having fun. More than fun, as a matter of fact. He looked as if he was having the time of his life.

"See?" Alex said, slumping back down beside Carrie and nudging her. "I told you they'd come alive if we made some noise."

Carrie nodded. The Panthers looked alive, all right. But she still didn't feel so thrilled. No . . . as Jordan ran up and down the court—patting Johnny Bates on the shoulder, grinning at Chris Tanzell—all her original fears came flooding back. A little over a week ago Jordan would have never even *talked* to those guys. Now he was obviously tight with them. He looked and sounded just like them—the way he was sweating and grunting in his black uniform. Everyone on the Panthers was the same. Including Jordan. He *was* a jock.

*He's never going to be the way he was before,* she said grimly to herself. *The more he hangs out with those guys, the more of a jerk he's going to become. Of course I'm afraid of change—if it means losing my best friend.*

She sighed and leaned forward, propping her elbows on her knees and resting her chin in the palms of her hands. It was sad. Watching Jordan play was almost like looking at an old photograph of a friend who had moved away. She could look at him—but the old Jordan, the one whom Sam had been talking about yesterday on Sky's boat—was long gone.

"What's wrong?" Sky murmured.

Carrie glanced up with a start. *Uh-oh.* She hadn't even noticed she wasn't watching the game anymore. She was totally spacing out, staring at the heavy black laces of her combat boots. "Huh?" she asked sheepishly.

Sky's forehead grew creased. "You look totally bummed right now."

Carrie shrugged and slouched back in her seat. "I guess I'm having a hard time getting into this basketball thing," she mumbled.

Sky's brown eyes flickered over Carrie's face. "That's not what's bumming you out, though," she prodded. "I can tell."

"Jeez," Carrie said dryly. She mustered a smile. "I've got to work harder on my lying skills."

"You *can't* lie around me," Sky said with a smirk. "You'd never get away with it. Now, what's up?"

Carrie took a deep breath. "It's just that . . . I know the letter I wrote was way too harsh. But still, it wasn't completely wrong. I mean, Jordan *is* a jock." She waved a hand at the basketball court. "Just look at him. He's becoming just like Chris and Johnny and the rest of those jerks."

Sky's eyes narrowed. "In what way?"

"In *every* way," Carrie replied glumly. She shook her head. "He's playing basketball, isn't he?"

Sky leaned back and raised her eyebrows.

"So playing basketball automatically makes you a jerk?"

"No . . . but if you're on the team, then you become a jock," Carrie stated slowly. "And once you become a jock, it isn't too long before you become a jerk."

Sky bit her lip—then burst out laughing.

Carrie frowned. "What's so funny?" she demanded.

"Carrie, listen to yourself!" Sky cried. "You're being totally prejudiced. You're basically saying that anyone on any basketball team is a jerk."

Carrie raised her shoulders. "Isn't it true?" she muttered, avoiding Sky's eyes.

"*What* are you saying?" Alex cut in.

"Carrie thinks that anybody who plays basketball is a jerk," Sky announced.

"That's *not* true." Carrie groaned, rolling her eyes. "I was just saying—"

"What about Matt?" Alex cut in. "*He* plays basketball. But you don't think *he's* a jerk. It's like that word you used in your letter. . . ." She scratched her wool cap. "Stereo . . ."

"Stereotype," Carrie finished.

"Exactly," Alex stated, pointing her finger. "You're stereotyping him."

"You guys—can we talk about this later?" Sam grumbled. "I'm trying to watch the game. We're here to watch Jordan, remember?"

Carrie didn't say anything. Alex was right, of course. Alex's brother, Matt, wasn't a jerk. And Carrie *was* stereotyping him. But Matt didn't really count. He was a year older, for one thing. He was in high school, for Pete's sake. He'd grown up and moved way beyond immature morons like Chris and Johnny.

"Look at it this way," Sky whispered, leaning toward Carrie's ear. "You know how the Amys always rag on you for wearing black all the time? Like you're a mental case or something?"

Carrie shifted uncomfortably in her seat. "What does *that* have to do with anything?" she asked.

"Because you're doing the same thing that *they* always do," Sky explained. "They think they know everything about you just because you wear black. They come up with all of these lame ideas about you for no reason at all. Don't you see? You're doing the same thing with all the guys on the basketball team." Her voice rose a little. "You don't even really *know* those guys. But I bet they're not all bad, right?"

*Whoa.* For a moment Carrie was too stunned to do anything but stare at Sky. *Was* she being like the Amys? She'd never thought about it that way. But she couldn't deny it. Every word out of Sky's mouth had been completely true. Making all kinds of judgments about those guys on the team—just because they happened to enjoy bouncing a lousy ball around—was no different than what the Amys did to her on a daily basis. She shuddered, suddenly feeling as if she were covered with some kind of diseased slime.

"See what I mean?" Sky prompted.

Carrie swallowed. "Yeah," she muttered. "I do."

"Look, I've got an idea," Sky went on. "After you watch the game, you write another letter to the editor, okay? Only *this* time you say that you were totally wrong to be prejudiced against jocks, and that basketball is actually kind of a cool sport, and that Jordan deserves to feel proud because he's such an amazing player."

Carrie thought for a moment. Incredibly enough, Sky's suggestion wasn't that outrageous. In a way it kind of made sense. The first letter had done a lot of damage—more damage than Carrie could have ever possibly imagined. So what could undo the damage—except another letter?

"What do you think?" Sky asked.

"I think you may be on to something," Carrie murmured. She nodded. Sky *was* on to something. Carrie's doubts began to disappear. Writing something for the paper could work. Because this time she would actually use her whole brain before she started to write—not just the angry part. As a matter of fact, she could even take her plan one step further than writing an editorial. Yeah. She could do something so totally crazy, so totally *unlike* anything she'd ever done before, that every single person at Robert Lowell would be completely blown away.

*Particularly* Jordan.

"So you'll do it?" Sky asked excitedly.

"I'll do something even better," Carrie stated. She smiled. "The *Observer* doesn't have an official sports column, right?"

"Uh . . . I don't think so," Sky said. "Why?"

"Because I'm going to make it my business to become Robert Lowell's first official sportswriter."

Sky started giggling.

Carrie wrinkled her brow. "What's so funny?"

"Carrie—you *hate* sports," Sky answered plainly. "Besides, you don't know a single thing about basketball. Coming to watch a game is one thing. You don't have to know anything about it to watch it—or even pretend like you're having a good time. But the thought of *you* writing a sports column is like . . . like *me* writing a meat-lovers' cookbook."

Carrie shook her head. "But that's the beauty of it!" she cried. "Don't you see? People will be totally shocked. And that's what I'm going for. It's exactly what you and Alex were talking about. People have this opinion about me—that I don't care about

67

sports. But I'm going to break my own stereotype. I'm going to show the world that Carrie Mersel is not afraid of change."

"Afraid of change?" Alex said, raising her eyebrows. "Where did *that* come from?"

Carrie felt her face flush. "Jordan said I blew everything out of proportion because I'm afraid of change."

"When did you talk to Jordan?" Sky asked.

"I called him last night to apologize. He wasn't exactly thrilled to hear from me," Carrie said. "He said I live in a cave." Carrie hung her head slightly.

Alex and Sky burst out laughing.

"It's not funny, you guys!" Carrie protested. "And I'm going to show him he's totally wrong. And writing a sports article is the way to do it."

Sky controlled her laughter. "I don't know," she finally mumbled. "I mean, all the articles have to be in to the Amys by the end of the day tomorrow. Even if they *let* you write a sports column, how will you learn all the rules and stuff in time?"

Carrie grinned. "Come on, Sky. How hard can the rules be? You put the ball in the basket. Anyway, if morons like Chris Tanzell and Johnny Bates can learn all the rules, I'll be able to pick them up in no time." She laughed. "Trust me. I'm gonna be the best sports columnist Robert Lowell has ever seen. I'll write the article tomorrow during lunch. I just gotta figure out how to get it in the paper."

# Friday:

## Carrie's Ruthless Climb to the Top of the Newspaper Business

### MORNING

**8:46 A.M.** Carrie strolls into Principal Cashen's office, requesting permission to create a new sports column for the *Observer*. Principal Cashen is confused. It's a great idea—but judging from Carrie's last editorial, he thinks it's . . . well, a little strange. Maybe she should think it over.

**9:31 A.M.** Carrie returns to Principal Cashen's office. She's thought it over. She promises she won't insult the players. After protesting for several minutes, Principal Cashen finally agrees. But Carrie still has to get approval from the editors in chief: Amy Anderson, Aimee Stewart, and Mel Eng.

**10:15 A.M.** Carrie spots Mel Eng in the hall by the lockers. She informs Mel that

Principal Cashen desperately wants Carrie to become a sports columnist. Mel shrugs. It's fine with her. It's one less thing *she'll* have to do.

*11:43 A.M.* Carrie bumps into Amy Anderson outside English class. She announces that she's going to write a sports column. Mel practically begged her to do it. Amy agrees—as long as Carrie swears she'll never talk to Amy in public again.

## AFTERNOON

*12:30 P.M.* Carrie skips lunch and proceeds to the library, where she checks out a basketball rule book titled *Rules of the Game*. Unfortunately it's the size of a large dictionary. Oh, well. She doesn't need it, anyway. She'll just improvise her article.

*1:17 P.M.* Carrie finds Aimee Stewart in the courtyard and states that she's about to become sports columnist for the *Observer*. She's going to write about yesterday's game. Aimee snorts. Does Carrie even *know* anything about sports?

*2:29 P.M.* Carrie finds Aimee again. Carrie insists that she knows *tons* about basketball. Jordan taught her. After all, *she's* been friends with Jordan Sullivan her whole life . . . unlike *some* people.

*3:15 P.M.* Aimee finally agrees to let Carrie write her stupid column. As long as it's all right with Amy Anderson, it's all right with her.

*3:16 P.M.* Carrie dashes back to Principal Cashen's office, stating that the editors in chief have given her their wholehearted support.

*3:19 P.M.* Carrie submits her article to the Amys. Amy Anderson frowns. That was pretty quick, wasn't it? Carrie didn't even know she had a column until five minutes ago. She wrote it in five minutes? Carrie shrugs nonchalantly. What can she say? She works fast.

# Nine

The moment Carrie got home Friday afternoon, she flopped down on her bed, snatched up the phone, and punched in Sky's number. "Guess what?" she said as soon as Sky answered. "You're talking to the *Robert Lowell Observer*'s newest sports columnist. I just submitted my first article."

Sky laughed. "Wow. *That* was fast."

Carrie snickered. "That's exactly what Amy Anderson said."

"Well . . . I guess I should congratulate you," Sky said slowly. "How did the article turn out?"

"Just wait till you see it," Carrie gushed, unable to contain her excitement. She sat up in bed and stared through a crack in the velvet curtains at the overcast skies outside. The weather might be lousy—but for the first time since her falling-out with Jordan, the dark clouds didn't match her mood. Nope. She was completely psyched. "Jordan is going to *freak*."

"I'll bet," Sky said quickly. "But I was just thinking . . ."

Carrie's eyes narrowed. There was a scheming tone in Sky's voice—a tone that usually spelled trouble. "What? What's wrong?"

"Nothing," Sky replied. "Except . . . I was just thinking about what you said the other day—Jordan saying you're afraid of change."

"Yeah . . . ," Carrie prompted.

"Well, I was thinking that you could do something else, too. You know, something that will show Jordan that you're totally behind him, like, one hundred percent. That your attitude has really shifted."

"Something else, huh?" Carrie raised her eyebrows, feeling wary. She could tell by Sky's eager voice that she already had something in mind. "Like what?"

"Why don't you change your look?" Sky said.

Carrie bit her lip. For a moment she wondered if she'd heard Sky correctly. "Change my *look*?" she asked.

"Yeah. Stop wearing combat boots. Wear another color besides black. Don't dye your hair—"

"Please," Carrie cut in dryly. "You're starting to sound exactly like my mom."

Sky giggled. "No, no. I'm being serious. Try going for a sporty-type thing. I mean, after all, you *are* a sports reporter, right? And if you do *that*, then you can show Jordan that you can do other things, *drastic* kinds of things—but still be your same old self. Just like he is. Does that make any sense?"

Carrie blinked a few times. "I'm not sure."

Sky cleared her throat. "What I'm saying is that you should give yourself a makeover."

Carrie's eyes bulged. A *makeover?* All right. Either Sky had recently developed a very bizarre sense of humor, or she had gone completely nutty.

"Carrie?" Sky prodded in the silence.

"A makeover," Carrie finally managed, trying not to laugh. "Like those girls in the Sweet Valley High books?"

Sky laughed. "Come on—"

"I don't believe this," Carrie muttered, twirling the phone cord around her fingers. She shivered—partly from a sudden chill and partly from the thought of changing her wardrobe. "You're serious, aren't you?"

"Just try it, all right?" Sky urged. Carrie could tell her friend was getting excited. "It'll be totally fun. It's supposed to rain tomorrow. We can go to the mall and load up on all kinds of great stuff. What better way to spend a rainy day than at the mall?"

Carrie didn't bother to answer. She could think of about a thousand better ways to spend a rainy day. But this *would* be something drastic. It might even be kind of amusing—in a very twisted way, of course.

"What do you say?" Sky prodded eagerly.

"Well . . ." Carrie turned the possibility over in her mind. Maybe Sky had a point. If Carrie did go for a "sporty-type thing," as Sky put it, then Jordan would be sure to notice. It would drive the point of the article home. He would see that she had changed her mind about jocks. He would see that she was taking her job as a reporter seriously—and not just doing it to make up for the letter.

"It'll be fu-un," Sky promised in a singsong voice.

Carrie chuckled. Shopping for a makeover. Jeez. Jordan had better believe she was serious about saving their friendship after something like this.

"Sure," she finally agreed. "Why not?"

# Carrie's
# Nine-Step Makeover

### Step One:
### Saturday Afternoon (the Mall)

Under Sky's careful instruction, Carrie purchases a pair of blue jeans, a bunch of totally lame sweatshirts (totally lame in Carrie's opinion, anyway), a Supersonics cap like the one Alex used to own . . . and yes, a pair of those painfully trendy high-heeled sneakers she swore she would *never* buy.

### Step Two:
### Sunday Evening (the Bathroom)

Carrie spends over an hour in the shower, frantically scrubbing black dye out of her hair. When she wipes the steam from the mirror, she sees her hair in all its long, natural chestnut glory for the first time in over five months. She screams.

## Step Three:
## Monday Morning (the Breakfast)

Carrie strolls into the kitchen in her new red sweatshirt, jeans, and sneakers. Her dye-free hair is in a high ponytail. When Mrs. Mersel sees her, she bursts into tears. "My prayers have been answered," she whispers. Carrie fights the temptation to throw all her new clothes into the trash compactor.

## Step Four:
## Monday Morning (the Bus)

The moment Carrie climbs on board the bus, everybody falls silent. Once again Jordan is sitting with Amy Anderson. He gasps when he sees Carrie. Finally Brick breaks the silence by asking: "It isn't Halloween yet, is it?"

## Step Five:
## Monday Afternoon (the Cafeteria)

At the lunch table Carrie calmly explains her new look to Alex, Sam, and Jordan—

who's still giving her the silent treatment. She's tired of the whole "goth-rock thing." What's the matter with trying out some new outfits? Jordan just looks at her as if she's lost her mind.

### Step Six:
### Monday Afternoon (the Hall)

Carrie spots Jordan outside French class. Finally she'll get a chance to talk to him. Unfortunately he's chatting with Johnny Bates and Chris Tanzell. Carrie calls to him. Jordan offers a feeble wave and hurries in the opposite direction.

### Step Seven:
### Monday Afternoon (the Bus)

Basketball practice is canceled. Jordan dashes for the bus and barely makes it. "Sit with us!" Aimee Stewart calls. Carrie waits in the back with Alex, Sam, and Sky. Carrie prays Jordan won't sit with the Amys. But after a furtive glance toward the back, Jordan slumps down beside Amy Anderson.

## Step Eight:
## Monday Night (the Phone Call)

Carrie calls Sky. It's very clear this makeover stuff is *not* working. Jordan hasn't said anything to her about how open-minded and accepting of change she is. In fact, he's still giving her the silent treatment. Sky explains that these things take time. It's only been one day—and the article hasn't even come out yet. Maybe Carrie should wear the Supersonics cap tomorrow.

## Step Nine:
## Tuesday Morning (the Last Straw)

Carrie boards the bus, wearing her Supersonics cap and a matching green sweatshirt. Much to her relief, Jordan is sitting in the backseat. But as soon as Carrie sits down, Jordan hops up, mumbling something about how it's "too crowded back here." He sits with the Amys for the rest of the ride to school. Alex asks Carrie if she can have the cap.

# Ten

Jordan plodded toward the cafeteria on Tuesday, feeling very much as if he were on his way to his own execution. Right at this very moment the newest issues of the *Observer* were being piled in the hall outside Principal Cashen's office. It would only be a matter of minutes before everyone had read Carrie's latest contribution. It would only be a matter of minutes before Jordan was humiliated before the entire school. *Again.*

How did this fight even start? He had no idea. All he knew was that Carrie wouldn't let it go. No . . . she had to become the *Observer*'s first sports columnist. He shook his head. Obviously that first editorial hadn't been enough. Carrie wanted more. She wanted to publicly rag on Jordan on a regular basis—week after week after week.

Why else had she bothered coming to

the game on Thursday? And why else did she keep wearing those incredibly freakish clothes? He didn't even feel like he *knew* her anymore. And he could just picture the first headline, too. Sullivan Stinks. *Oh, man*. Maybe he should just cut his losses and leave school right now.

"Hey, Sullivan!" a voice shouted behind him.

*Here goes*. Jordan slowly turned around. Chris Tanzell was storming through the hall. He had a rolled-up newspaper clenched tightly in his fist. *Uh-oh*.

"You wanna tell me what's going on here?" Chris yelled, shoving the paper into Jordan's hand. "Where do you get off with this stuff?"

Jordan swallowed. "Uh . . . what stuff?" he mumbled confusedly, unrolling the paper. His fingers were trembling. He'd never *seen* Chris so mad. "I haven't seen the paper yet—"

"Don't even try it," Chris snapped. "I'm not stupid."

*Not compared to most household pets*, Jordan thought, but he kept his mouth shut. His eyes scanned the page. "Sullivan

Wows Sheridan School." He frowned. *That* was the headline? That wasn't so bad. . . .

"You got your weird little friend to ignore the rest of the team, didn't you?" Chris growled. "Pretty swift, Sullivan. Only a dork like you would pull something like that."

Jordan had no idea what Chris was talking about. He shook his head and read the article.

### Sullivan Wows Sheridan School
#### by Carrie Mersel

Like Vikings on the rampage, the Robert Lowell Panthers took no prisoners at Sheridan School this past Thursday.

The Panthers played superior basketball in every possible way, breezing to an easy forty-eight to thirty-two victory over the Bulls. Led once again by the brilliant play of Jordan Sullivan, they established a lead quickly in the first half. They never looked back. Sullivan's passing, shooting, and all-around hustle gave the Panthers the edge they needed throughout the entire game.

The Bulls were no match for Sullivan's trademark outside shot. Sullivan scored the final basket of the game, dazzling his opponents. Defensively he played a superb game as well. The Bulls' efforts to score were consistently thwarted by Sullivan. In the end they were broken, intimidated, and humiliated—and they had Jordan Sullivan to thank.

Does this mean that Sullivan will lead the Panthers to this year's championship? Probably. With Jordan Sullivan on the Panthers' side, it's hard to see how anything can possibly go wrong.

Come to the Panthers next home game against the Edgevale Hawks! Watch Sullivan in action!

Blood rushed to Jordan's face. He didn't know *what* to make of this. Part of him was flattered. But mostly he was embarrassed. Alarmed, even. Carrie hadn't mentioned any other player. Why? Jordan had played a decent game—but not *that* great. Why was the article entirely about *him?*

"It didn't even say that I was the leading scorer!" Chris yelled. "Sullivan, you hardly even *played* during the second half!"

Jordan glanced up. *Oh, jeez.* A crowd had started to gather around them— including Johnny Bates and a few other guys from the team. They all had papers. This was about to get ugly. Really ugly.

"Hey, Sullivan?" Johnny called to him. "What does *rampage* mean?"

"That's what we're gonna do to his

85

face," Chris spat, snatching the paper out of Jordan's hands. "You know, you got some nerve—"

"I had nothing to do with this," Jordan pleaded. He knew he sounded amazingly desperate and wimpy, but he couldn't help it. "I swear. Find Carrie and ask her. I mean it. I haven't even *spoken* to her in days. She did this all on her own. Just ask her."

Chris sneered. "Yeah. Like she's really gonna tell the truth."

"Well, uh . . . I don't know what to tell you," Jordan stuttered, stepping back. "She—"

"This is the biggest load of crap I've ever *seen!*" Johnny suddenly shouted. He hurled the paper to the floor. "You can't play defense at all, Sullivan!"

Jordan flinched. His eyes darted anxiously around the hall. Five or six guys were glaring at him now. This might be a good opportunity to make a run for it. He whirled—then slammed right into a mass of blond curls.

"Whoa, there!" a giggling voice squealed.

It was Aimee. Great. Perfect timing.

"Sorry," he mumbled, trying to push past her.

"Hey! Where are you going?" She grabbed onto his arm—then smiled at Chris and Johnny and the others. For some bizarre reason she was seemingly oblivious to the fact that they were about to pound Jordan into the floor. "What's up? What do you guys think of the article?"

"Oh, we just think it's *peachy*," Johnny grumbled sarcastically.

Chris snickered. "Yeah. We *loved* reading about a guy who sat on the bench for half the game."

Aimee raised her eyebrows. "Jealous, boys?" she teased.

*Jealous?* Jordan cringed. That wasn't going to make them happy. He forced a strained smile. "Look, I know the article was a little one-sided," he said quickly. "But there's nothing any of us can do about it now. So let's just eat lunch and forget about it. Huh?"

"Don't be so modest," Aimee scolded, letting his arm go. "If you were the star, you were the star." She laughed once.

"Your teammates will deal with it. No, the only problem with the article was Carrie's writing. You have to admit, it's *terrible*. Personally I think I could have done a much better job, but . . ."

*Please shut up*, Jordan begged silently. Aimee could be a real pain in the neck sometimes. None of the Amys ever knew when to keep quiet.

"The point is, you should be proud of yourself," Aimee finished.

Jordan nodded. "Right," he muttered. He started inching toward the cafeteria doors.

"Hey, Sullivan," Johnny called. He shook his head, grinning. "You're wrong about something."

"I am?" he croaked.

"Yeah. You said there's nothing we can do about it." His big, toothy grin widened. "And that's not true. We *are* gonna do something about it. You can count on it."

# Eleven

"So did anyone find out what Jordan thought about the article?" Alex asked as she rummaged through the Mersels' refrigerator after school on Tuesday. "I didn't get a chance to talk to him all day."

"Neither did I," Carrie mumbled. She kicked her feet under the kitchen table. She was too antsy to sit still. Her high-heeled sneakers made little screeching noises on the white tile floor. She was definitely going to have to get rid of these sneakers. They were way too loud. "The only time I saw him was when he poked his head into the cafeteria. It was almost as if he disappeared after that." She glanced across the table at Sky and Sam. "Did you guys talk to him?"

Sky shook her head. "Not me."

"Me neither," Sam muttered. His dark brow grew furrowed. He leaned back in the chair and stared off into space. "It's weird. I *always* talk to him after sixth period. But today when he saw me in the hall, he just took off in the other direction. He looked kind of freaked, too."

Carrie chewed her lip, frowning. This was not good. She was starting to get seriously worried. He must have read the article, but why would he be upset? He should have come running to thank her. She had been sure that this stupid fight would be over by now. What more could she possibly do?

"Maybe he's starting to get sick of all the attention," Alex suggested. She closed the refrigerator door and opened the freezer. "Maybe he wants to keep a really low profile or something." She reached for a carton of chocolate chocolate chip ice cream. "You know—like Michael Jackson."

Carrie smirked. "Michael Jackson?"

"Yeah." Alex plopped down at the table and began spooning ice cream straight from the box. "You know how Michael Jackson is really shy?" she asked with her mouth half full. "He hides from people all the time. There's a word for it. He's a . . . um . . ."

"Weirdo?" Sky suggested, grinning.

Alex shrugged. "Well, *that*, too. But I was thinking—"

"Recluse," Carrie finished.

Alex pointed her spoon at Carrie. "Bingo!"

Sam shook his head. "You guys, there's no *way* Jordan is keeping a low profile, or becoming a recluse, or anything like that. Come on." He laughed. "If anybody loves attention, it's Jordan."

"So what's going on?" Carrie asked, almost to herself. "It doesn't make any sense."

Sky sighed. "Well, *I* think that Jordan . . . that Jordan—" She broke off. A piercing, high-pitched *beep-beep-beep* had suddenly filled the room.

Carrie rolled her eyes.

"What *is* that?" Sky asked, giggling.

"The phone," Carrie mumbled. She pushed herself up. There was no use explaining. Her mom had just gotten this brand-new cordless phone that sounded like a burglar alarm. Why? Carrie had no idea. She sighed and lifted the receiver off the wall. It was probably her mom right now, calling to announce that she was being held up at some vitally important meeting of the Gourmet Club.

"Hello?" Carrie asked flatly.

"It's Jordan."

Carrie nearly dropped the phone.

"Hello?" came the voice at the other end.

Everybody at the table stared at her.

"Who is it?" Alex whispered.

Carrie cupped a shaky hand over the mouthpiece. "Jordan!" she hissed.

"Jordan?" they all cried at once.

"Shhh!" Carrie removed her hand and turned toward the wall. "Hi," she breathed. Her heart was fluttering. "What, uh . . . what's up?"

"What's up?" He chuckled. "Not much. What's up with you? Long time, no talk."

"No kidding," Carrie muttered. She couldn't read the tone of his voice. Was he angry? Joking around? It was impossible to tell.

"Right . . . uh, anyway, I read the sports column in the *Observer* today," Jordan said. "I guess I should thank you."

Carrie shifted on her feet. He didn't *sound* as if he wanted to thank her. In fact, he sounded as if thanking her was about the last thing he wanted to do. "You're welcome," she said carefully.

There was a pause. "So. What made you want to write a *sports* column?"

Carrie hesitated. "I . . . uh, I realized that my editorial letter was a little harsh. The guys on the team aren't that bad," she answered. "I wanted to make up for it."

Jordan chuckled again. "That's funny. I don't know if you *were* wrong about the guys on the team."

"You *don't*?" Carrie frowned. "What do you mean?"

"Well, I think you were right about certain things," he said evenly. "Jocks *are* a little egotistical. It turns out they're also stupid."

Carrie's eyes narrowed. What was going on here? "Um, Jordan—"

"You see, a couple of the more stupid, egotistical guys on the team are a little mad," he went on. "They actually think that I *made* you write that article."

"They *what?*" Carrie cried. "Jordan, I didn't—"

"Let me finish," Jordan interrupted calmly. "The problem is, they don't understand why they weren't included in the sports column. I mean, some guys on the team played much better than I did. They played more minutes. They scored more points. So they're a little confused. And so am I."

Carrie drew in her breath. She couldn't believe this. "Jordan, I . . . uh, I guess I wasn't paying as much attention to the other guys as I should have," she mumbled, struggling to organize her thoughts. "I . . . uh . . . how mad are they?"

"You don't want to know," Jordan muttered.

"Well, well—what can I *do?*" she asked frantically.

"I'm not really sure," he replied. "Let me just ask you something, though. You weren't *trying* to make them mad, were you? I mean, you didn't do this on purpose . . . you know, to get me back or anything?"

"Of *course* not!" Carrie exclaimed. "I did it because . . . ." She held her breath. What could she possibly say? "I did it because I was sorry and I was worried you were never going to talk to me again," she finally admitted.

He sighed. "Well, I guess it worked, then. You got me to talk to you again."

Carrie gulped. "Jordan—you aren't still mad at me, are you?" she murmured.

He didn't reply.

"Jordan?"

"Now's probably not the best time to ask me that," he grumbled.

She winced. How could he be so mean? "I'm *sorry!*" she cried desperately. "What do you want me to say?"

"I don't know," he moaned. "All I know is that my entire team wants to kill me because you left them out of your article."

"Well, the next time I'll include them," she promised. "I swear."

"Okay, okay." His tone softened a little. "Listen, you know we have a game against Edgevale on Thursday, right? Just tell the truth about the game. That's all I want you to do."

"You got it," she breathed hoarsely.

"Good. I'll talk to you later, Carrie. Good-bye." The line clicked.

Carrie blinked. Was that it? After all that time, all the energy she'd spent, all the effort she'd gone to in order to make him believe that she wasn't afraid of change, Jordan *still* hadn't forgiven her. On the other hand, she couldn't really blame him. If ten hulking meatheads wanted to pulverize *her*—well, she might feel the same way. She hung up the phone and slowly turned to face the others.

All three of her friends were gazing at her, waiting.

"So?" Sky eventually asked. "Did you guys make up?"

Carrie shrugged. "I don't really know," she said with a sigh. "But the way I see it, I have one last chance. I'll know after Thursday's game."

# Twelve

## I

Carrie was starting to get nervous.

The Panthers were losing. They were actually *losing*.

In all her worries about today's game—over how she would compliment each and every member of the team, over how she would learn all the rules by this afternoon, over how she wouldn't make a lifelong enemy of Jordan—she never once considered the possibility that the Panthers might lose.

How on earth could she write a beautiful, glowing article about a loss?

She glanced around the gym. The bleachers were totally silent. Everybody was wearing the exact same grim, stone-faced expression—including Alex, Sam, and Sky. The atmosphere was even worse than it had been at Sheridan School. At least *that* gym had been empty. But this gym was packed, and nobody was talking. Even the Amys hadn't so much as uttered a peep. Carrie rubbed her hands on her blue jeans. Her legs were so *itchy* in these things. Maybe she should just treat the whole game like one of her horror stories. There didn't seem to be much difference.

The whistle blew for a time-out.

"Hey, Carrie?" Sky said. "Can I ask you something?"

Carrie shrugged. "Sure."

"Why isn't anybody passing the ball to Jordan?"

"I don't know," Carrie lied. But she knew very well why. She just didn't want to admit it—to herself or to anyone else. The guys on the team weren't passing the ball to Jordan because they were majorly angry with him. And it was all her fault.

"Looks to me like they're doing it on purpose," Sam muttered.

"On *purpose?*" Sky frowned. "But why?"

Sam shrugged. "Beats me."

Carrie slumped deep into her seat. At least they didn't know the truth. She could hardly bear to watch. Even if everybody on the team was mad, losing didn't make any sense. Jordan was a good player. When time was running out, you were supposed to use your good players.

She glanced at the scoreboard. Only two minutes were left.

So why couldn't the guys on the team just stop acting like morons for once and get Jordan the ball?

## II

"All right, guys, listen up," Coach Powell snarled. "In case you haven't noticed, we're down by six points. What the heck is your problem?"

Jordan groaned inwardly. He was exhausted. Sweat bathed his face and arms. His lungs were heaving. And even though he'd been running around like crazy out there, nobody seemed to notice he was even on the court. Nobody had thrown the ball to him. Not once. He was actually a little ticked off himself. So what if they were mad about Carrie's article? Didn't they want to win?

"Hey, Tanzell—are you daydreaming or something?" Coach Powell asked. He jerked a thumb at Jordan. "Sullivan here has been wide open about a dozen times." His voice hardened. "When he's open . . . *throw him the ball.*"

Chris lifted his shoulders. He didn't seem the least bit concerned. "Sorry," he muttered.

"You better be," Coach Powell grumbled. He picked up a little chalkboard and began drawing Xs and Os. "Now here's what I want you to do. . . ."

Jordan shot a quick, nasty look at Chris.

But Chris just smiled.

And in that instant Jordan knew that Chris *wasn't* going to throw him the ball. Ever. Even if it meant losing the game. Jordan's teammates *didn't* want to win.

## III

"Let's go, Panthers!" Carrie shouted along with the crowd. *Finally* it seemed as if the people in the bleachers were showing some signs of life. Maybe they could breathe some life into the players, too. The Panthers could still win, couldn't they? They were only down by six points. Anything was possible. "Let's go, Panthers!"

Carrie kept her eyes pinned to Jordan. He was scrambling across court, waving his hands furiously. Johnny Bates was dribbling the ball. But he didn't even *look* in Jordan's direction. Instead he threw up a wild shot that completely missed the net. The ball bounced out of bounds.

A whistle blew.

Carrie's jaw tightened. *That's it,* she said to herself. *Maybe I started it—but this whole thing has gone way too far.* She cupped her hands over her mouth and took a huge breath.

"Hey, *stupid!*" she shrieked. A few people in the stands turned to look at her—but she didn't care. She was furious. If the Panthers were going to win, they *had* to get the ball to Jordan. "Johnny Bates!"

Johnny paused for a moment on the floor and squinted in Carrie's direction.

"Yeah, *you!*" Carrie hooted. "Instead of taking a lame shot, why don't you pass it? There's no *i* in *team,* dummy!"

Alex, Sky, and Sam giggled. But they were the only ones laughing. Everybody else looked mortified. Except for the guys who were playing for Edgevale, of course. *They* seemed to think it was funny.

"That's an *awesome* line," Alex stated.

"Totally," Sky agreed. "Did you make that up?"

For a moment Carrie was tempted to take credit for it. But then she shrugged. "Nope. It was the only thing I learned from that book—*Rules of the Game*," she said.

## IV

Jordan allowed himself a little smile as he ran back down the court. *No i in team.* It was Coach Powell's favorite expression. He had to hand it to Carrie—she always knew *exactly* what to say. He glanced at Johnny. The guy was fuming.

Jordan couldn't have been happier.

If his teammates hated him, fine. He could handle the nasty looks in the locker room. But they were freezing him out of the game. When Johnny took that pathetic shot instead of passing the ball to Jordan, it was confirmed. Aimee was right. They *were* jealous. So to get revenge, they were pretending as if Jordan wasn't even on the team. They were willing to lose just for the sake of making Jordan mad.

How lame was *that*?

Jordan struggled to get into his defensive position—but before he could, Edgevale scored another basket. The score was now forty-four to thirty-six.

Jordan glanced at the clock. Less than a minute remained.

The game was pretty much over.

Oh, well. At this point Jordan didn't even care. Why would he even want to play on this team? Basketball wasn't worth this much trouble. It was supposed to be fun.

He should have trusted his instincts. He had known right from the start that he didn't fit in with these guys. The Robert Lowell Panthers were all a bunch of fools. Come to think of it, Carrie had been right, too. The players on this team did think they were better than everyone else. They sure thought that they were better than Jordan.

So there wasn't much point in playing with them, was there?

## V

Even when the final buzzer sounded, Carrie still couldn't quite believe that the Panthers had lost. Sure, deep down she knew the game was over. She knew they'd been beaten. But for some reason it just didn't seem to make sense. Maybe it was because she hadn't seen them lose until now. She didn't know. She could only stand there, gazing at the scoreboard while people quietly filed out of the gym.

"Carrie?" Sky murmured, tugging on the sleeve of her sweater. "You coming?"

Finally Carrie allowed her head to droop. "Yeah." She sighed. "I'm coming."

"I can't believe they ignored Jordan that whole time," Sam muttered. "They would have won if they hadn't ignored him."

"I know." Carrie groaned. "I know."

"Hey, Carrie—look at it this way," Alex offered. "At least you won't have any problem focusing on other guys besides Jordan for your article. Jordan had nothing to *do* with this game."

Carrie nodded. Alex was right. Jordan might as well have been in another time zone. She *couldn't* write about him.

But the whole reason she'd even invented this stupid sports column was for Jordan. If he wasn't involved, she had absolutely no interest. None. In fact, the thought of heaping false praise on Chris Tanzell and Johnny Bates was enough to turn her stomach. They had *cost* Robert Lowell the game.

She didn't want to make Jordan mad . . . but at the same time could he blame her for despising the guys who'd treated him like garbage?

No. She didn't think he could.

And that meant there was only one thing left to do.

# Thirteen

"So let me get this straight," Principal Cashen said, leaning back in his leather chair. "You want to stop writing for the *Robert Lowell Observer*."

"That's right," Carrie replied.

He stared at his desk for a moment. "Does Amy, Mel, or Aimee know anything about this?"

Carrie shook her head. "No, Principal Cashen. I haven't told them yet. In fact, I just made up my mind yesterday afternoon after the game. But I doubt they'll mind."

He glanced up. "What makes you think they won't mind?"

Carrie shrugged. How could she answer that? *Because they hate my guts and the feeling is mutual?* No—that wouldn't do. "Well, to tell you the truth, we don't see eye to eye on a lot of things," she said.

Principal Cashen nodded gravely. Carrie squirmed in her hard-backed wooden chair. She never understood why there was no couch in here. Shouldn't a big-time principal have a couch in his office? This place was definitely big enough for a couch. Of course, there was probably a reason. Maybe he *wanted* people to be uncomfortable. That was probably why he kept his office dark, too— like all the rest of the teachers at Robert Lowell. It was like they were all vampires or something.

"Can I ask you a question, Carrie?" he said after a moment.

"Sure," Carrie replied, even though she was a little nervous. Whenever somebody asked if they could ask you something instead of just asking the question, you *knew* it was going to be bad.

"Why did you want to write a sports column at all?"

Carrie just stared at him. Yup. That was bad. She couldn't blame him, though. After all, Jordan had asked her the same thing.

"Carrie?" Principal Cashen coaxed.

"I—uh, I thought it might be fun," she managed, smiling anxiously. "I figured it would be a change from the kind of stuff I usually write. Plus I thought I could write about sports differently than most people because . . . um . . . because—"

"Because you're not interested in sports?" Principal Cashen finished dryly.

Carrie's face reddened. *Oh, brother.* She should have known he'd see right through her. He *was* smart. She always managed to forget that. As terrible as it seemed, she had a hard time taking a pudgy, balding guy in a really corny suit all that seriously.

"I don't mean to put you on the spot," Principal Cashen said. He cleared his throat. The faint beginnings of a smile curled on his lips. "May I make a suggestion, though?"

"Sure," Carrie mumbled, looking at her lap.

"Why don't you write something *else* for the paper? Why don't you create a column that really interests you?"

Carrie's head jerked up. "You'd let me do that?" she asked, baffled.

Principal Cashen chuckled softly. "Yes, Carrie, I would. Principals aren't ogres, you know. We're in the business of educating and encouraging young people." He raised his eyebrows. "If you can believe it."

"No, no—I didn't . . . um, I mean—"

"Look, the point is that you're a talented writer," he gently interrupted. "I was very pleased when you expressed an interest in writing for the *Observer*. I just think you need to direct your energies in the right place."

Carrie shook her head, too overcome with a strange mixture of gratitude, shock, and embarrassment to speak. Finally she took a deep breath. "That's . . . uh, nice of you to say," she murmured.

He shrugged. "It's true."

Carrie met his gaze. "What kind of a column could it be?" she asked curiously.

"That's up to you," he replied.

"Hmmm." She smiled. "I don't know if the Amys—I mean, Amy Anderson and the others—would be too thrilled about my writing a column."

"Why not? They let you write a sports column, didn't they?" Principal Cashen leaned back in his chair. "Besides, I think it's a good idea for the *Observer* to have . . .

well, differing points of view. Amy and her friends tend to be pretty one-sided about things. Even if they aren't thrilled, they'll have to live with it." His face grew stern. "Of course, anything you contribute *does* have to be in good taste."

"Of course," Carrie replied quickly. Her smile widened. "Well, I don't know how I can refuse after that. You've got yourself a columnist."

"Good." He pushed back his chair and gestured toward the door. "I don't want you to be late for your bus. We can discuss the specifics later."

Carrie hopped out of her chair. "Sure. Thanks a lot, Principal Cashen. I mean it."

"Oh—there's one more quick thing, too," he announced, holding up his finger. "You're friends with Jordan Sullivan, right?"

Her stomach abruptly twisted into a knot. In all the talk about the column, she'd totally forgotten that Jordan was the reason she was here in the first place. *Was* she friends with Jordan Sullivan? She didn't even know how to answer that question. "Why?"

"Because I was very impressed with

that self-portrait he drew for Aimee's article," he said in a businesslike tone. "I was thinking that it would be wonderful if he wanted to contribute drawings to the *Observer* on a regular basis. If you see him, just mention it to him."

Carrie nodded. *Wow,* she thought. Jordan would *love* a regular cartoon. Or would he? The knot faded, leaving an odd emptiness in its place. She didn't even know anymore. She and Jordan didn't even *speak* to each other anymore. Whenever he saw her these days, he just stared at her as if she were a total lunatic.

"I'll tell him," she finally murmured. *But I don't know if he'll even listen to me,* she added silently.

No. It was time for this silliness to end. He'd have to listen to her. She'd make sure of it. In fact, she would go to his house this very afternoon. She'd wait there for him until he was done with basketball practice. She wouldn't let one more day pass without a face-to-face talk. They'd grown too far apart.

If he wanted to keep playing basketball, fine. That was part of who he was. But he couldn't forget the other parts. He couldn't go around pretending to be somebody else. After all, *she'd* learned that she couldn't be somebody else, right? She was no sports columnist. She never was. She was just herself, for better or worse. Jordan would just have to deal with it.

Just like Carrie would have to deal with his basketball.

If she could learn to deal, so could he.

# Fourteen

"You want to *what?*" Coach Powell cried.

"I want to quit the team," Jordan repeated quietly, standing as straight as he could in front of Coach Powell's desk.

Coach Powell leaned forward and looked Jordan directly in the eye. He took a deep breath. His forehead grew wrinkled, as if he were thinking very hard about what he wanted to say. "Is something bothering you, Jordan?" he asked. "Do you want to talk about it?"

Jordan shrugged, but he was struck by something. Coach Powell had never called him by his first name before. It made Jordan feel more relaxed, somehow. And that was good, considering that he could hardly breathe in here. But it was almost as if Coach Powell were finally admitting that Jordan was an actual living, breathing *person*. It was kind of nice.

"I just don't think I'm cut out to play on this team," Jordan said simply. "That's all."

Coach Powell nodded. "You're upset about yesterday's game, right?"

Jordan lowered his gaze. "A little," he admitted.

"Well, that's perfectly understandable," Coach Powell stated. "Listen. I don't know what's going on between you and the other guys on the team, but whatever it is, I'm sure we can work it out—"

"There's really nothing to work out, Coach Powell," Jordan interrupted as politely as he could. He lifted his head and brushed his bangs out of his eyes. "I appreciate it and all, but nothing's going to change how I feel."

Coach Powell leaned back in his chair and gave his head a thoughtful scratch. "Is something *specific* bothering you?"

*Yeah*, Jordan thought. *The whole team. They make me ill.* He paused. There had to be a more delicate way to explain things. But explaining things had never been his strong point. He suddenly wished Carrie were here. *She* could tell him what to say. Nobody else had a better way with words. Like what she'd said to Johnny . . .

"Well, let me put it this way," he said after a few seconds. "You know how you're always telling us that there's no *i* in *team*?"

Coach Powell's eyes narrowed. "Yes?"

"I just think . . . I think that the guys on the team really wish that were true," Jordan finished awkwardly. "That *I* wasn't part of the team. You know what I mean?"

All of a sudden Coach Powell burst into laughter: "Ahee, hee, hee!"

Jordan's eyes widened. He wasn't trying to be funny. He'd never seen Coach Powell laugh before, either. It was kind of scary.

"You know what, Jordan?" Coach Powell asked, shaking his head. "You may be one of the smartest players ever to walk in here."

Jordan blinked a few times. "What?"

"It's true." He laughed again. "You know—if half the guys on the team used their brains as much as you do, we'd be guaranteed to win the championship."

Jordan just stared at him. *Jeez.* He was shocked. This wasn't like Coach Powell at all. He handed out compliments about as often as the cafeteria handed out edible food. Jordan had no idea what to say. In fact, he was starting to get a little embarrassed. He started backing toward the door. "Well, thanks for your time. I really should be going. I have to catch the bus—"

"Wait!" Coach Powell raised his hands. "Just hold on one more second. Look, I know that some of the guys have a hard time sharing the spotlight. But try to see things from their point of view. Most of them have been playing together for the past three years. You just joined the team a few weeks ago. There's bound to be some tension, right? They're not *all* bad, Jordan. They're just human."

Jordan started shaking his head. Human? That would be pushing it a little in Johnny and Chris's case. "I know what you're trying to say," he said. "But really, my mind is made up." He reached for the doorknob. "Thanks again."

Coach Powell sighed and folded his hands across his lap. "All right. If your mind is made up, it's made up. But we really could use you, Jordan. You've got a lot of talent." He pointed a finger at his head. "Especially up here."

"Thanks," Jordan mumbled. Now he

was *really* embarrassed. He pushed open the door.

"But do me a favor, okay?" Coach Powell asked.

Jordan hesitated in the doorway. "What's that?"

"Join the basketball team when you get to high school." He flashed a wry grin. "Somebody's gotta keep all your older brothers in line."

Jordan chuckled. "You got it."

"Good. I'll see you later, Jordan."

"See ya." He closed the office door behind him.

*Wow.* Jordan wandered out into the crowded hallway, shaking his head. Kids bumped into him as they ran toward the front doors, but he hardly noticed.

He couldn't believe how painless that had been. He'd been dreading that confrontation all day. But Coach Powell totally understood where he was coming from. He didn't get angry or act disappointed—or even try to push Jordan into staying. He *knew* Jordan would have been miserable on that team. And he respected Jordan's decision.

That was pretty cool.

"Hello? Jordan Sullivan? Anybody home?"

He glanced up. Aimee was right there.

*Oh yeah.* He'd told her to wait for him outside Coach Powell's office. He wanted her to be the first to know that he'd quit.

"Hey," he said. "Sorry. I'm kind of spaced right now."

Aimee raised her eyebrows. "I noticed." She giggled. "By the way, you're walking in the wrong direction. Basketball practice is *that* way."

"But I'm not going to basketball practice," he replied with a smile.

"Why not?" She stared at him. "Are you sick or something?"

"Not at all." He laughed. "In fact, I haven't felt this good in a long time. I just quit the team."

Aimee froze. "You *what?*" she cried.

"I quit," he said casually. "It's no big deal—"

"But *why?*" she demanded. "Did somebody make you?"

Jordan paused. "No," he said, a little taken aback. That was sort of a weird question. "I just wasn't happy," he explained. "I'd rather shoot hoops with my friends on my own time than practice every day. And playing on that team meant hanging out with—"

He broke off. Aimee's face was all shriveled—as if she'd just taken a bite of some really old cottage cheese or something. She looked disgusted.

"What's the matter?" he asked.

"Jordan—playing on that team is the best thing that ever happened to you!" she snapped. "You can't just quit!"

Jordan frowned. "I can't?"

Aimee put her hands on her hips and rolled her eyes. "Of course not, *stupid.* Don't you see? If you quit the team, you go back to being what you were before." She sneered. "No, even worse. Quitters are the lowest forms of low. Quitters are losers."

Jordan just gaped at her. For a second he almost felt like laughing. Coach Powell wasn't mad, but Aimee Stewart was. Either she was insane, or stupid, or incredibly conceited—or all of the above. Did she honestly think that those words would make him want to rush back and join the Panthers? "And what was I *before?*" he asked.

"You know what I mean," she muttered.

"No." He smiled. "No—please explain it to me." He had a feeling he knew *exactly* what she meant—but he wanted her to say the words herself.

She glowered at him. "If you quit, you go back to being just another a *dork*, like all the rest of your dumb friends."

Jordan nodded. *Ah, yes.* Aimee thought that basketball was the only thing in Jordan's life that saved him from being a hopeless failure.

But he'd always kind of known what Aimee thought.

He knew something else now, too. He *would* go back to being like all his dumb friends if he quit the team. Yes—once again Aimee was absolutely right. And if quitting the team made him a dork in her eyes . . . hey, he could live with that. Plus he'd have the added bonus of never having to talk to her again. Carrie would be proud. That's because Carrie was a true friend. She'd made a fool out of Johnny Bates in front of the entire school—all for Jordan. She'd always hated the whole idea of basketball, anyway.

Or did she?

Jordan sighed. Who knew what Carrie was thinking these days? She had told him that she was writing the sports column to apologize for being so harsh in her first letter. But what was up with her hair? And the jeans and sweatshirts and baseball caps. What was *that* all about?

*I have to talk to her. I have to get everything out in the open once and for all.*

Without another word he turned and hurried toward the front doors. He couldn't afford to miss the bus. Not today.

"Where do you think you're going!" Aimee shouted after him. "I haven't finished talking to you yet."

"That's okay," he called over his shoulder. "You wouldn't want to talk to me, anyway. I'm going back to being a dork."

# Fifteen

Carrie didn't think she'd *ever* felt more lonely or self-conscious. Nope. The backseat was totally empty. Well, except for *her*, of course. She'd sunk as low as a person could sink. She was hunched in the backseat of bus number four, staring down at a pair of heinous high-heeled sneakers. It was like a form of torture or something. Why couldn't Brick just start the lousy engine and get out of here?

Maybe she should have gone with Alex, Sam, and Sky. They were on their way to the high school to watch Alex's brother play basketball right now. But Carrie had refused to go. After all, she'd seen enough basketball to last the rest of her life and beyond.

As usual, of course, she hadn't been thinking. Anything was better than this. She had never realized how huge this seat was. She could lie down across it if she wanted to. Actually, that might not be a bad idea.

"Hey, man!" Brick called. "I didn't expect to see *you*."

*What now?* Carrie thought dismally. She raised her eyes.

"Jordan!" she gasped.

Her mouth fell open. What was he doing here?

He marched down the aisle and slumped beside her. His bangs immediately fell in his eyes. He brushed them aside and smiled. "What's up?"

For a moment she was unable to speak. She just shook her head. This was impossible.

He peered at her closely. "What's the matter?"

"I . . . I don't get it," she murmured at last. "Why aren't you at practice?"

"Would you believe me if I told you that I quit the team?" he asked.

Carrie struggled for a moment to process his words. Quit the team? "No," she answered. "I wouldn't."

He laughed. "That seems to be what *everybody* thinks."

"Hey, Jordan!" Brick yelled from up front. "Are you here to stay or what? I've gotta start this thing."

"Go ahead," Jordan called.

The bus roared to life and bounced out of the semicircular driveway.

Only then did it hit Carrie: *He really must have quit.* Why else would he have stayed on the bus?

"What made you do it?" she asked, unable to tear her eyes from him.

He shrugged, slouching in the seat. "*You* saw the game yesterday," he mumbled. "If the guys on the team don't want me to—"

"Jordan, I have something to tell you," Carrie suddenly blurted. "I can't write a fair article about yesterday's game like you asked me to. I can't write anything more about the guys on the team, or the game, or anything having to do with basketball."

Jordan hesitated, staring at her. Afternoon sunlight flickered across his face as the bus began the long climb up Pike's Way. "You can't?" he finally asked.

She shook her head. "No. I'm not the sports columnist anymore."

"Whoa." He sat up straight. "What happened?"

She grinned slightly. "The same thing that happened to you. I quit."

"You *did?*" he exclaimed.

"I had to." She turned and gazed out the window at the passing pine trees. "You know that old saying, If you don't have something nice to say, don't say anything at all?" she muttered. "That's a very polite way of summing up how I feel about the Robert Lowell Panthers. I had nothing nice to say. So there was no way I could keep writing a sports column."

"Yeah, after what happened yesterday, I'm not exactly having happy thoughts about the team, either," Jordan said ruefully. "It's so annoying. It turned out those guys actually fit the stupid stereotypes."

"What do you mean?" Carrie asked.

Jordan shifted in his seat. "When I was having fun and playing well, the guys didn't seem so bad," Jordan said. "But when they got angry about your article, they wouldn't even let me explain. They turned into total meatheads, just like you said."

"So all jocks *are* jerks?" Carrie asked, confused.

"No, not at all," Jordan answered. "I mean, I'm still thinking about playing on the high school team next year because I really do love basketball, and I'm sure some of the guys will be cool. It's just a lot of the guys on the Panthers do happen to be, well, *really* stupid."

Carrie laughed once. "You can say that again. I couldn't believe the way they were freezing you out." She shook her head. "But guess what? I have some incredible news."

"What is it?" Jordan asked, looking interested.

"I went to Principal Cashen's office to quit the paper for good. But he ended up convincing me to stay. He says I can write my own column." She flashed a wicked smile. "About *anything*."

Jordan's face brightened. "Carrie, that's *awesome!*"

"That's not all, though," she went on, unable to wipe the smile from her face. "He told me to tell *you* that he wants you to start doing cartoons for the *Observer* on a regular basis."

Jordan drew back his head. "Get out of here."

"I'm *serious*," she said. "He saw that self-portrait you did. He said he was really impressed."

Jordan didn't say anything for what

seemed like a long time. He just kept glancing at her, then at the floor, then back.

"What?" she asked worriedly. "Aren't you psyched?"

"Listen, Carrie, you're not pulling my leg, are you?" he asked cautiously.

"Pulling your leg?" Carrie cried. "Are you *kidding*?"

"Well, to tell you the truth, I don't know *what* to think anymore," Jordan murmured. His bangs fell in his face as he lowered his eyes again. "I mean, I hardly feel like I know you right now, you know? Everything is so *weird.*"

Carrie nodded. For a moment she was half tempted to throw her arms around him and hug him as tightly as possible. But she managed to control herself. After all, she didn't want him to gag or anything. She took a deep breath. "I was feeling the same thing about you. That's how this whole thing started, remember? I was freaked out by the way you were acting like a total superstar and hanging out with the Amys—"

"Don't remind me," Jordan interrupted, grimacing. "I mean, I can't believe I actually hung out with Aimee Stewart. As Sky would say: *Eww.*"

Carrie grinned. "Actually, she did say that. . . ."

"The point is that it's over," he piped up. "I'm willing to forget about that letter you wrote if you're willing to forget that I ever hung out with Aimee Stewart." He extended a hand. "Deal?"

Carrie grasped his hand and shook it so vigorously that Jordan's entire body wriggled. "Deal."

"Whoa!" he yelped.

"Oops." Carrie let his hand go. "Sorry."

"Can I ask you something, though?" Jordan brushed his bangs aside and looked her in the eye. "Why did you decide to stop dyeing your hair?"

Carrie blushed slightly. "What? You don't like the natural look?"

"No, no . . . it's not that," he said quickly. "The natural look . . . is, um, interesting."

"Yeah, right," Carrie muttered with a smirk. "You sound about as convincing as one of those infomercials for dandruff shampoo."

Jordan chuckled. "You're right. I guess I kind of miss the old Carrie, you know? That's what freaked me out so much. The way you totally changed."

"Wait a minute," Carrie said, sitting up straight. "*You* were freaked by the way *I* changed. What're you, like, living in the *Ice Age*?"

Jordan brought his hands to his face. "Ugh!" he groaned. "I can't believe I said that to you the other day! I was just so mad. You can wear whatever you want. We're still friends even if you never wear black again."

"Really?" Carrie asked. She pointed down at her horrible high-heeled sneakers. "Well, what do you think of these?"

Jordan didn't say anything. His smile was totally forced.

"My thoughts exactly," Carrie stated. "In fact . . ." She reached under her seat, yanked the laces untied, and wrenched the sneakers from her feet. Then she calmly placed them at her side. She wiggled her toes in her socks. "Ahhh," she said, closing her eyes. "That's *sooo* much better."

"I couldn't agree with you more." Jordan sighed and leaned back in his seat.

"There's one more thing, too," he said solemnly.

"What?" Carrie asked.

Jordan bit his lip. "No matter what

either of us does in the future—I mean, even if one of us decides to take up sumo wrestling or something—let's promise that we'll always be friends."

"And we'll never, ever say that one of us fits a stereotype again," Carrie added.

"Never," Jordan agreed.

Carrie smiled, even though at the moment she felt like bursting into tears—not that she would allow herself to do anything so gushy. Jordan would think she was crazy. But it was pretty amazing that even when they'd been drifting apart, they'd both been feeling the same things about each other. It was almost like there was a psychic bond between them or something. *Oh, brother.* Now she was starting to think like one of those tabloid magazines. Maybe she *was* crazy.

"Promise?" Jordan asked.

"Promise," Carrie managed after a moment.

"Good. So . . . Principal C. really liked my drawing?" Jordan asked.

Carrie threw her hands in the air. "Yes!" she exclaimed, laughing. "*Jeez.* How many times do I have to tell you?"

Jordan cocked an eyebrow. "Just making

sure." He looked out the window. The bus was turning off Pike's Way onto Whidbey Road. Before Carrie knew it, the bus squealed to a stop in front of an enormous, disgustingly modern white house. *Yikes*. She couldn't believe it. She was already *home*. She jumped up and snatched her sneakers off the seat. "I guess I'll see you—"

"Hey!" Jordan suddenly cried. "I got it!"

Carrie hesitated. "Got what?"

"Why don't you and I do something for the paper *together?*" His face brightened. "You can write the column—and I'll draw the illustrations. What do you think?"

"What do I *think?*" Carrie laughed. "Genius. Pure genius. What do you have in mind?"

Jordan tilted his head and wrinkled his brow. "I don't know."

Carrie thought for a second. There was no way they could figure out something right this second. She glanced around the bus. Her eyes happened to fall on the pair of sneakers in her hand. She'd have to save these for Halloween.

*Hold on.*

That was it! Not the sneakers—but what

they represented. Namely being a poser. She didn't have to wait for Halloween. The sneakers were *already* part of a costume Carrie had worn. They represented all the stupid stuff she'd done these past couple of weeks—all the roles she'd tried to play and failed at playing. How could she have ever worn these? They were so *ugly*. Oh, well. It didn't matter. What mattered was that if Jordan could forgive her for the sneakers, he could forgive her for anything.

"Maybe it should be about all the posers at our school," she suggested slowly. "You know, all the people who try to be something they aren't." She raised her eyebrows. "After all, it's something we're both familiar with, right?"

Jordan's green eyes sparkled. "You bet . . ."

"So what do you say we get started?" She reached out and yanked him up. Excitement was bubbling up inside her. This was going to be good. After all, they were the two most brilliant kids at Robert Lowell, right? Well, maybe not. But who cared? They were *partners*.

"It's time to seize the day, my man. Opportunity is knocking!"

# Poser Patrol

**by Carrie Mersel
and
Jordan Sullivan**

Yes, folks—it's that time of year again.

It's the time of year when the days get a little shorter. The time when the wind blows a little colder. And the time when certain members of the student body (who shall remain nameless for the sake of their protection) lose their minds and start acting like total idiots.

As you may or may not know, this problem has a clinical name. It's called "posing." And it affects at least two out of every five members of the Robert Lowell student body.

Perhaps you think we're exaggerating.

Hardly. As two former posers, we're in a perfect position to evaluate others. You see, *we've* both been down that dark road. *We've* both lost our minds. So it's only fair that we perform a public service and describe these terrifying symptoms in our fellow students.

Take the case of a certain girl we all know and love. We'll call her Bootsy. Anyway, Bootsy recently had a huge crush on a certain boy with certain, shall we say . . . talents. She *worshiped* him.

But as soon as this boy found out that certain people with similar talents happened to be total jerks (who shall also remain nameless), he decided to keep his talents to himself.

Then—poof! Bootsy suddenly forgot that he existed.

Strange, isn't it?

Does she still really like him? Doubtful. Did she ever like him? Questionable. Did she only pretend to like him because it made her look good? Now *there's* an idea. . . .

Sadly, we cannot answer these questions with absolute certainty.

After careful study we've come to the conclusion that Bootsy is too confused to answer them herself.

Watch out! You could be next. And trust us, nobody wants to be like Bootsy.

# Collect all the titles in the MAKING FRIENDS series!

The prices shown below are correct at the time of going to press. However, Macmillan Publishers reserve the right to show new retail prices on covers which may differ from those previously advertised.

All MAKING FRIENDS titles can be ordered at your local bookshop or are available by post from:

**Book Service by Post**
**PO Box 29, Douglas, Isle of Man IM99 1BQ**

Credit cards accepted. For details:
Telephone: 01624 675137
Fax: 01624 670923
E-mail: bookshop@enterprise.net

**Free postage and packing in the UK.**
Overseas customers: add £1 per book (paperback)
and £3 per book (hardback).